"You can't do this…"

"This is about protecting what is mine." Rakhal was completely unmoved by her dramatics, for she was starting to beat him with her hands, but he captured her wrists.

"Why are you doing this to me?"

"Because I could not leave you at your home.… If you are pregnant with my child, then I need to be certain you are taking care of yourself and will do nothing to jeopardize its existence. You will stay in the palace, where you'll be well looked after."

"Where will you be?"

"In the desert. Soon I am to take a wife, it is right that I go there for contemplation and meditation, while we wait to see the outcome with you. You will be well taken care of, you will be tended to, and if you are not pregnant, of course you can come back home."

"And if I am?" Natasha begged, but already she knew the answer.

"If you are pregnant," so matter of fact was his voice as he said it, as her heart hammered in her chest, "then there is no question that we will marry."

Empire of the Sands

One powerful legacy, two desert kings

For rival sheikhs Rakhal and Emir, kingdom comes first, last and always.

But underneath their steely control lies an unfathomable passion—deeper than an oasis and hotter than the scorching desert sun.

By day they rule with an iron fist, but by night, under a blanket of diamond-like stars, pleasure reigns!

Banished to the Harem

Playboy Sheikh Rakhal has time for one more fling in London before he must return to his kingdom, Alzirz—and there's room in his harem for beautiful Natasha Winters!

November 2012

Emir, ruler of Alzan, is preparing to marry again. Nanny Amy may meet his exacting requirements in the bedroom, but is she suitable to be the sheikh's wife?

Look out for Emir's story coming soon!

Carol Marinelli

BANISHED TO THE HAREM

Empire of the Sands

HARLEQUIN®

entertain, enrich, inspire™

Recycling programs
for this product may
not exist in your area.

ISBN-13: 978-0-373-23867-5

BANISHED TO THE HAREM

Copyright © 2012 by Carol Marinelli

All about the author…
Carol Marinelli

CAROL MARINELLI finds writing a bio rather like writing her New Years Resolutions. Oh, she'd love to say that since she wrote the last one, she now goes to the gym regularly and doesn't stop for coffee and cake and a gossip afterwards; that she's incredibly organized and writes for a few productive hours a day after tidying her immaculate house and a brisk walk with the dog.

The reality is, Carol spends an inordinate amount of time daydreaming about dark, brooding men and exotic places (research), which doesn't leave too much time for the gym, housework or anything that comes in between. Her most productive writing hours happen to be in the middle of the night, which leaves her in a constant state of bewildered exhaustion.

Originally from England, Carol now lives in Melbourne, Australia. She adores going back to the UK for a visit—actually, she adores going anywhere for a visit—and constantly (expensively) strives to overcome her fear of flying. She has three gorgeous children who are growing up so fast (too fast—they've just worked out that she lies about her age!) and keep her busy with a never-ending round of homework, sport and friends coming over.

A nurse and a writer, Carol writes for the Harlequin® Presents and Medical Romance lines and is passionate about both. She loves the fast-paced, busy setting of a modern hospital, but, every now and then admits it's bliss to escape to the glamorous, alluring world of her Presents heroes and heroines. A bit like her real life actually!

Other titles by Carol Marinelli available in eBook:

Harlequin Presents®

PROLOGUE

'I SHALL return on Monday.' Crown Prince Sheikh Rakhal Alzirz would not be swayed. 'Now, onto other matters.'

'But the King has requested that you leave London immediately.'

Rakhal's jaw tightened as Abdul pressed on. It was rare indeed for Abdul to persist when Rakhal had made his feelings clear on a subject, for Rakhal was not a man who changed his mind often—nor did he take orders from an aide—even his most senior one. But in this case Abdul was relaying orders that came directly from the King, which forced him to be bold.

'The King is most insistent that you return to Alzirz by tomorrow. He will not hear otherwise.'

'I shall speak with my father myself,'

Rakhal said. 'I am not simply going to walk away at his bidding.'

'The King is unwell, though….' Abdul closed his eyes for a moment, grief and worry evident on his face.

'Which is why I shall be married before the month's end,' Rakhal interrupted. 'I accept that it is important for our people to have the security of knowing the Crown Prince is married, especially with the King now ill, however…'

Rakhal did not finish his sentence. He did not need to explain himself to Abdul, so again he changed the subject, his black eyes daring Abdul not join him this time.

'Now, onto other matters.' He did not wait for his aide's nod. 'We need to discuss a suitable gift to celebrate this morning's news from Alzan. I want to express my delight to Sheikh King Emir Alzan.' A dark smile twisted at the edge of Rakhal's full lips, for despite the news about his father's health, despite the summons for him to return to Alzirz and choose a bride, the week had at least brought one piece of good news.

In fact two pieces of good news!

'Something very pink,' Rakhal said, and for the first time that morning Abdul smiled too, for it was good news indeed. The birth of female twins in Alzan gave the Kingdom of Alzirz some much-needed breathing space. Not much, for undoubtedly Emir and his wife would soon produce a son, but for now there was reason to smile.

Long ago Alzirz and Alzan had been one country—Alzanirz—but there had been much unrest and the Sultan at the time had sought a solution. A mix-up at the birth of his identical twin sons had provided him with one, and on his death the Kingdom of Alzanirz had been divided between his sons.

It was a temporary solution—at least temporary in desert terms—for the mathematicians and predictors of the time had all agreed that in years, or even hundreds of years, the two countries would again become one. It could be no other way, because a special law had been designed for each country that meant one day they would be reunited. Each country had been given one law by which they must abide, and only the opposing ruler could revoke it.

In Alzirz, where Rakhal would soon be King, the ruler could take but one wedded partner in their lifetime, and his firstborn, whether boy or girl, would be heir.

Rakhal's mother, Layla, weak and thin and grieving her Bedouin life, had died birthing Rakhal, her only child, and the country had held its breath as the tiny, premature infant struggled to hold on to life. For a while it had seemed that the predictions of old were coming true, and that the Kingdom of Alzirz would be handed over to Alzan's rule—for how could a baby born so early, a baby so tiny, possibly survive?

But Rakhal had not only survived. Out of the starvation of his mother's womb he had thrived.

In Alzan the one rule was different— there the King could marry again on the death of his wife, but the ruler of Alzan must always be male. And now, as of this morning, Emir was the father of two little girls. Oh, there would be much celebrating and dancing in Alzirz tonight—their country was safe.

For now.

Having entered his third decade, Rakhal could no longer put it off. He had rowed frequently about this with his father, but now accepted that it was time for him to choose his bride. A wife he would bed at her fertile times only, for she would be rested at other times. A wife he would see only for copulation and at formal functions or special occasions. She would live a luxurious, pampered life in her own area of the palace, and guide the raising of children he would barely see.

Emir would see *his* children.... Rakhal recognised the darkness that dwelled within him as he thought of his rival, but it did not enter his head that jealousy might reside there too—for Rakhal knew that he had everything.

'Do you have any ideas as to a gift?' Abdul broke into Rakhal's thoughts.

'Two pink diamonds, perhaps?' Rakhal mused. 'No.' He changed his mind. 'I need to think about this. I want something more subtle than diamonds—something that will make him churn as he receives it.' Of course he and Emir were polite when they met, but there was a deep rivalry between them—a rivalry that had existed before either was born and would be passed on for generations to come. 'For once I will enjoy choosing a gift.'

'Very well,' Abdul said, gathering up his papers and preparing to leave the study in Rakhal's luxurious hotel suite. But as he got to the door he could not help himself from asking, 'You *will* speak with the King?'

Rakhal dismissed him with a wave of his hand. He did not answer to his aide—he had said that he would speak to the King, and that was enough.

Rakhal did speak with his father. He was the only person in Alzirz who was not intimidated by the King.

'You are to return this instant,' the King demanded. 'The people are becoming unsettled and need to know that you have chosen your bride. I wish to go to my grave knowing you shall produce an heir. You are to return and marry.'

'Of course,' Rakhal responded calmly, because there was no debating that point. But he refused to dance to his father's tune—they were two strong and proud men and often clashed. Both had been born natural leaders, and neither liked to be told what to do, yet there was another reason that Rakhal stood his ground and told his father he would not return till Monday. If he boarded a plane immediately, if he gave in without protest, then his father would really know that he was dying.

And he *was* dying.

Hanging up the phone, Rakhal closed his eyes and rested his head on his hands for a moment. He had spoken at length yesterday with the royal doctor and he knew more than the King did. His father had but a few months to live.

Conversations with his father were always difficult, always stilted. As a child Rakhal had been brought up by the maidens, and had seen his father only on special occasions. Once, as a teenager, he had joined his father in the desert and learnt the teachings of old. Now, though, as leadership approached for Rakhal, his father seemed to want to discuss his every move.

It was one of the reasons Rakhal liked London. He liked the freedom of this strange land, where women talked about making love and demanded things from their partner that were not necessary in Al-zirz. He wanted to linger just a little longer.

Rakhal had a deep affinity for the city that was, of course, never discussed. Only by chance had Rakhal found out that it was here in this hotel that he had been conceived—a break with desert rules that had not only cost his mother her life, but also threatened the very country he would soon rule.

He stood and headed to the window and looked at the grey view, at the misty rain and the cluttered streets. He could not wholly fathom this country's appeal, for he knew it was the desert where he belonged, the desert he must return to.

The desert that was summoning him home.

CHAPTER ONE

THE policewoman could not have been more bored as she instructed Natasha to fill out the necessary forms.

And, yes, in the scheme of things it wasn't exactly riveting that her car had been stolen, and neither was it a disaster, but on the back of everything else that she was dealing with, today of all days, Natasha could very easily have put her head on the desk and wept.

She didn't, of course. Natasha just got on with what she had to—it was how this year had been. Her long, thick red hair was wet from the rain and dripped on the counter as she bent her head. She pushed it out of her eyes. Her fingers were white from the cold. If her car *had* to have been stolen, Natasha almost wished it could have been in a couple of days' time, when she would have known nothing about it.

Natasha was supposed to be spending this gruelling day planning a holiday. It was the anniversary of her parents' death, and she had wanted to mark it somehow. She had been determined to push on with her life, but had finally listened when her friends had said that she needed a break— a proper one—and it didn't need to be expensive.

As a substitute teacher it had been easy for her to arrange a fortnight off, and today she had been planning to visit the cemetery and then go to a friend's house to book the cheapest, hottest place on the planet she could afford. Instead she was standing in a draughty police station, politely trying not to listen as the woman beside her reported a domestic incident.

The policewoman's voice suddenly trailed off mid-sentence. In fact the whole room seemed to stop, even the argument breaking out between a father and son paused, and Natasha looked up as a door beside the counter opened.

She watched the policewoman's cheeks

redden, and as Natasha followed her gaze she could certainly see why. Walking into the foyer was possibly the most beautiful man she had ever seen.

Definitely the most beautiful, she amended, as he walked past the counter and came into full view. He was tall, with exotic dark looks, his elegance so effortless that he wore even a torn shirt and a black eye well.

He was tousled and unshaven, and the torn shirt allowed for more than a glimpse of one broad coffee-coloured shoulder. As he gave up trying to fasten the broken buttons on his shirt he moved to tuck it in, and even though Natasha looked away the image of a flat stomach with a snake of jet hair danced before her eyes. She struggled to remember the registration number of the car she'd owned for more than five years.

'Maybe you should go and sit down to fill it in?' the policewoman suggested.

Natasha was quite sure she was only being helpful because, now he had moved, Natasha was blocking her view of the exotic prisoner. Still, it was rather nice to sit in a front row seat and every now and then look up from the form to witness him sliding in his belt and buckling it, and then, a moment later, when they were handed to him, slipping on his shoes.

'Are you sure we can't offer you a ride home?' a sergeant asked.

'That won't be necessary.'

His voice was deep and low and richly accented, and despite the circumstances he was very much the one in command—there was an air of haughtiness to him as he took his jacket from the sergeant and brushed it down before putting it on. The gesture, as some dust fell to the floor, was curiously insolent, as if telling all present that he was better than this.

'We really are sorry for the mix-up...' the sergeant continued.

Natasha quickly looked back to her paperwork as *he* made his way over to the bench where she sat, raised a foot and placed it beside her, and proceeded to lace up his shoe. There was a delicious waft that reached her nostrils, the last traces of cologne combined with the essence of male, and though she resisted, though she tried terribly hard not to, her body did what it had to and despite Natasha's best intentions she looked up.

Looked up into a face that was exquisite, into eyes that were at first black but, as she stared, became the indigo of a midnight sky. He let her explore the vastness, let her deep into the reaches of his gaze, then he withdrew that pleasure, his concentration moved back to his footwear and Natasha was for a second lost. So lost that she did not turn her face away, still watched, mouth slightly gaping, as his dark red lips tightened when the sergeant spoke on.

'As I said before, Your Highness…'

Natasha's mouth gaped fully open. No wonder the sergeant was groveling. There was a diplomatic incident unfolding right here in the room.

'…I can only apologise.'

'You were doing your job.' Shoes laced, he stood to his impressive height. 'I should not have been there in the first place. I understand that now. I did not at the time.' He looked down at the policeman and gave a brief nod—a nod that was final, that somehow confirmed he was giving his word. 'It is forgotten.' Relief flooded over the sergeant's face even as His Highness snapped his fingers. 'I need my phone.'

'Of course.'

Natasha was dying to know what had happened, what the mistake had been, but unfortunately she couldn't drag out filling in the form any longer, so she went up to the counter and handed it in. She could feel his dark eyes on her shoulders as she spoke with the policewoman, and as Natasha turned to go their eyes met briefly for the second time. Briefly because Natasha tore hers away, for there was a strange suggestion in his eyes that she could not logically explain.

'Good morning.'

His words were very deliberate and very much aimed at her. They forced her gaze to dart back to him as he greeted her in circumstances where it would be more customary to ignore another person. It was almost inappropriate to initiate a conversation here, and Natasha flushed as she returned his greeting.

'Morning...'

There was the slightest upturn to his mouth—imperceptible, almost, but there—

as if he found her voice pleasing, as if somehow he had won, for still he stared. There was a bizarre feeling of danger. Her heart was racing and her breathing was shallow and fast. Instinct told her to run—especially as that haughty mouth now shifted a little further, moved to almost a smile. There was a beckoning in it, and she understood now the danger. For her body still told her to run—except *to* him.

'Thank you.' Natasha turned to the policewoman, thanked her for her assistance, and then, because she had no choice, she walked past him to reach the exit.

It was an almost impossible task, for never had she been so aware—not just of him, but of her own body: the sound of her boots as she clipped past him, the relief in her nostrils as they once again detected him, the burn of his eyes as they unashamedly followed her progress. And, though she could not know, she was certain of the turn of his head as she passed him, and knew he was watching as she walked out through the door.

It was a relief to be out in the rain—never had she had a man so potent linger in his attention on her—and Natasha walked quickly from the police station, crossing at the lights and then breaking into a run when she saw her bus. It drove off as she approached it and she felt like banging on the door as it passed, even chased it for a futile few seconds, knowing what she would see now.

She tried not to look—tried to disappear in the empty bus shelter—but of course she could not. He walked out of the police station and down the steps in his slightly muddied tuxedo, and instead of turning up his collar, as most would, he lifted his face to the rain, closed his eyes and ran a hand over his face as if he were showering. He made a wet winter morning suddenly beautiful. He made the whole wretched day somehow worth it for that image alone. Natasha watched as he lifted his phone to his ear and then turned around. She realised he was disorientated as to his location, but he walked on a little farther and located the name of the suburb from the sign on the police station's wall.

No, he did not belong here.

He pocketed his phone and leant against

the wall. It was then that he caught her watching. She tried to pretend that she hadn't been. Deliberately Natasha didn't jerk her head away. Instead she let her gaze travel past him and then out into the street, willing another bus to appear, but she could see him in her peripheral vision. She knew that he had moved from the wall and, ignoring the pedestrian crossing, was walking very directly towards her. There were angry hoots from drivers as he halted the traffic and calmly took his time—it was Natasha's heart that was racing as he joined her in what once had been *her* shelter. Except it wasn't the rain Natasha needed sheltering from.

He stood just a little nearer to her than was polite. Natasha couldn't really explain why she felt that, because soon the shelter would fill up, and on a rainy morning like this one soon she and any number of strangers would be crammed in like sardines. But for now, while it was just the two of them, he was too close—especially when she knew, was quite sure, that he didn't need to be here. *His people* hadn't told His Highness that perhaps he should get the bus.

What was he doing here? her mind begged to know the answer to the question. What had the mistake been?

'The husband came home.'

His rich voice answered her unspoken question, and despite her best intentions to ignore him Natasha let out a small, almost nervous laugh, then turned her head to him. Immediate was the wish that she hadn't, that she had chosen simply to ignore him, because those eyes were waiting for her again—that face, that body, even his scent; he was almost too beautiful for conversation—better, perhaps, that he remain in her head as an image, a memory, rather than become tainted by truth.

Something deep inside warned Natasha that she should not engage with him, that it would be far safer to ignore him, but she couldn't, and her eyes found his mouth as he spoke on.

'He thought that I was in his house stealing.'

Rakhal looked into green eyes, saw a blush flood her face as it had when last their eyes had met—only this time there was a parting of her lips as she smiled. But that initial response was brief, for quickly, he noted, she changed her mind. The smile vanished and her words were terse.

'Technically, you were!'

She went back to looking out into the road and Rakhal fought with a rare need to explain himself. He knew what had happened last night did not put him in a flattering light, but given where they had met he felt it important that she knew the reason he had been locked up if he were to get to know her some more.

And of that Rakhal had every intention.

There was a very rare beauty to her. Redheads had never appealed to him, but this morning he found the colouring intriguing. Darkened by the rain, her hair ran in trails along her trenchcoat. He wanted to take a towel and rub it dry, to watch the golds and oranges emerge. He liked too the paleness of her skin that so readily displayed her passions; it was pinking now around her ears. He wanted her to turn again and face him—Rakhal wanted another glimpse of her green eyes.

'I did not know.' He watched her ears redden as he carried on the conversation. 'Of course that is no excuse.'

It was the reason he had assured the policemen he would not be taking things any further—because she was right: technically he had been stealing, and that did not sit well with Rakhal. He could surely live and die a hundred times trying to work out the rules of this land—there were wedding rings, but some chose not to wear them; there were titles, but some chose not to use them; there were, of course, women who chose to lie. And, in fairness to him, it was particularly confusing for Rakhal—for his heartbreaking looks assured that many a ring or a diamond were slipped into a purse when he entered a room. But instead of working out the rules, this morning he chose to work out this woman.

Direct was his approach.

'What were you at the police station for?'

She was tempted just to ignore him, but that would only serve to show him the impact he'd had on her, so she attempted to answer as if he were just another person at a bus stop, making idle conversation. 'My car was stolen.'

'That must be inconvenient,' Rakhal responded, watching her shoulders stiffen.

'Just a bit.' Natasha bristled, because it was far more than *inconvenient*, but then if he was royal, if he was as well-off as his appearance indicated, perhaps having his car stolen *would* be a mere inconvenience. But maybe she was being a bit rude. He had done nothing wrong, after all. It was her private response to him that was inappropriate. 'I was supposed to be going on holiday...'

'A driving holiday?'

She laughed. Perish the thought! 'No.' She turned just a little towards him. It seemed rude to keep talking over her shoulder. 'Overseas.'

Those gorgeous eyes narrowed into a frown as he attempted to perceive the problem. 'Did you need your car to get you to the airport?'

It was easier just to nod and say yes, to turn away from him again and will the bus to hurry up.

They stood in silence as grumpy morning commuters forced him a little closer to her. She caught the scent of him again, and then, after a stretch of interminable silence, when it felt as if he were counting every hair on the back of her head, he resumed their conversation and very unexpectedly made her laugh.

'Couldn't you get a taxi?'

Now she turned and fully faced him. Now she accepted the conversation. Rakhal enjoyed the victory as much as he had enjoyed the small battle, for rarely was a woman unwilling, and never was there one he could not get to unbend.

'It's a little bit more complicated than that.'

It was *so* much more complicated than simply getting a taxi to the airport. Truth be told, she couldn't really afford a holiday anyway; she had lent her brother Mark so much money to help with his gambling debts. She had been hoping to take a break for her sanity more than anything else, because her brother's problems weren't going away any time soon. Still, this dashing stranger didn't need to know all about that—except he did not allow her to leave it there.

'In what way?'

He dragged out a conversation, Natasha recognised. He persisted when others would not. 'It just is.'

Still he frowned. Still he clearly expected her to tell.

Tell a man she had never met? Tell a man she knew nothing about other than that he ignored social norms?

And he was ignoring them again now—as the lengthening bus queue jostled to fit beneath the shelter he placed a hand on her elbow, instead of keeping a respectable shred of distance as the crowd surged behind him, forming a shield around her. And if it appeared manly, it felt impolite.

As impolite as her own thoughts as his fingers wrapped around the sleeve of her coat. For there was a fleeting thought that if the queue were to surge again he might kiss her—a thought too dangerous to follow as her body pressed into him. She moved her arm, turned away from him, and was it regret or relief when she saw her bus?

Natasha put her arm out to hail it and so too did he. Except she quickly realised it wasn't the bus he was summoning—it was a black limousine, with all its windows darkened. The car indicated and started to slow down.

'Can I offer you a lift home?'

'No!' Her voice was panicked, though not from his offer. If the car stopped now then the bus wouldn't. 'It can't park there…'

He didn't understand her urgency, or was incapable of opening a car door himself, because he stood waiting till a man in robes climbed out and opened it for him. 'I insist,' he said.

'Just go,' Natasha begged, but it was already too late. The bus sailed happily past the stop blocked by his vehicle and Natasha heard the moans and protests from the angry queue behind her—not that it perturbed *him* in the least. 'You made me miss my bus!'

'Then I must give you a lift.'

And, yes, she knew she should not accept lifts from strangers—knew that this man had the strangest effect on her. She knew of many things in that instant—like the angry commuters she'd be left with, and the cold and the wet. Yes, there were reasons both to accept and to decline, and Natasha could justify either one.

She could never justify the real reason she stepped into the car, though—a need to prolong this chance meeting, a desire for her time with this exotic stranger not to end.

It was terribly warm inside, and there was Arabic music playing. The seat was sumptuous as she sank into it, and she felt as if she had entered another world—especially when a robed man handed her a small cup that had no handle. She could almost hear her mother warning her that she would be a fool to accept.

'It is tea,' she was informed by His Highness.

Yes, her mother might once have warned her, but she was twenty-four now, and after a slight hesitation she accepted the drink. It was sweet and fragrant, and it was much nicer to sit in luxurious comfort than to shiver at the bus stop. She certainly didn't relax, though—how could she with him sitting opposite her? With those black eyes waiting for her to look at him?

'Where do you live?'

She gave him her address—she had no choice but to do so; she had accepted a ride home after all.

'Forgive me,' he said. 'A few hours in a cell and I forget my manners.' His English, though good, was the only part of him that was less than perfect, and yet it made him more so somehow. 'I have not properly introduced myself. I am Sheikh Rakhal, Crown Prince of Alzirz.'

'Natasha Winters.' There was not much she could add to that, but his haughty, beautiful face did yield a small smile when she said, 'Of London.'

Their conversation was somewhat awkward. He asked her where she had been intending to go on holiday, and seemed somewhat bemused by the concept of a travel agent or booking a holiday online. In turn he told her that he was in London for business, and that though he came here often soon he would be returning to his home.

'And now I return you to yours,' he said, as the car turned into her street and slowed down.

Somehow she knew things would not be left there.

'Would you care to join me for dinner tonight?' Rakhal asked. He did not await a response—after all the answer was inevitable. 'I'll pick you up at seven.'

'I'm sorry.' She shook her head. 'I've already got plans.' She flushed a little. She was clearly lying. She had no plans. She was supposed to be jetting off for two weeks and had told him as much. And she was tempted, but they had met in a police station and he was wearing a black eye from an aggrieved husband. It didn't take much to work out that he would want more than dinner.

And so too would she.

She was stunned at her reaction to him; never had a man affected her so. It was as if a pulse beat in the air between them— a tangible pulse that somehow connected them. There was a raw sexual energy to him, a restless prowess, and she dared not lower her guard for this man was far more of a man than she was used to, more male than she had ever encountered before. She reached for the door.

'Wait,' Rakhal said, reaching out his hand and capturing her wrist.

There was a flutter of panic that rose from her stomach to her throat at the thought that he might not let her out—or was that just the effect of contact, for his fingers were warm on her skin?

'You do not open the door.'

Neither, it would seem, did he, for the robed man who had served them tea was the one who climbed out. Rakhal's hand was still on her wrist and she waited. For what, she wasn't quite sure. Another offer of dinner? Or perhaps it was he who was waiting? Maybe he thought she would ask him inside?

She looked at that handsome face, at the mouth that was so sorely tempting, and then at his come-to-bed eyes. She could almost see them reflected there—could envisage them tumbling in her bed. It was a dangerous vision to have, so she pulled her wrist away. 'Thank you for the lift.'

He watched her almost run to her house,

saw her safely inside and then gestured to his driver to move on. They rode in silence.

Abdul knew better than to question why Rakhal had been at a police station, where the bruises were from—it was not an aide's place to question the Crown Prince. He would bring him a poultice later, and again over the next few days, in the hope that the bruises would be gone by his return to Alzirz.

Right now Rakhal had more than bruises and several hours in a prison cell on his mind. He had never been said no to before; quite simply it had never happened—but he did not grace the markets and had no need to barter. Rakhal knew she was not like the women he usually played with but, oh, the heaven of getting her to unbend. It was a shame he was leaving on Monday. She might be worth pursuing otherwise. Still, maybe the next time he visited London… Except he would be a married man by then, and something told him that Natasha would be even more disapproving.

He wished she had said yes.

Natasha thought the same almost as soon as she stepped inside. Away from him she

was far more logical—she had just turned
down a dinner invitation from surely the
most gorgeous man alive. The loss of her
holiday and her car seemed like minor in-
conveniences compared to what she had
just denied herself. She moved to the window and watched his car glide off. Her
hand moved to her wrist, where his fingers had been. She replayed their conversations again.

He had been nothing but polite, she told
herself. It was her mind that was depraved.

She kicked herself all day as she dealt
with the car insurance company, and then
tried to sound cheerful when one of her
friends rang to tell her they had secured
an amazing deal for ten nights in Tenerife.
They would be leaving tonight, and was
Natasha quite sure that she didn't want to
change her mind and join them?

Natasha almost did, but then she looked
down at the figure that had been quoted as
the excess on her insurance and regretfully
turned down her second amazing offer in
one day.

Her brother's debts were not Natasha's
responsibility, all her friends said, but actu-

ally they were. Natasha had not told anyone about the loan she had taken out for him—which was why her friends were unable to understand why she didn't want to come away on holiday with them, especially after such a hellish year.

To Mark's credit, since she had taken the loan he had always paid her back on time, and Natasha was starting to feel as if she could breathe, that maybe he was finally working things out. A payment was due tomorrow, and she pulled up her bank account online. Her emerging confidence in her brother vanished as she realised that his payment to her hadn't gone in, and immediately she rang him.

'You'll have it next week.'

Natasha closed her eyes as he reeled off excuses. 'It's not good enough, Mark, the payment's due tomorrow.' She cursed at the near miss—she might have been *en route* to Tenerife, not knowing that she had defaulted on a loan payment. 'I can't afford to cover it, Mark. I had my car stolen last night.' She would not cry, she was tougher than that, but for so many reasons today was especially hard. 'When I agreed to get this loan you promised you would never miss a payment.'

'I said you'll have it next week. There's nothing else I can do. Look,' he said, 'how soon till you get the car insurance payout?'

'Sorry?'

'You said your car had been stolen,' Mark said. 'You'll get that payment soon. That will cover it.'

'It might be found,' Natasha said. 'And if it isn't the payout will buy me another car.' But, even though there was so much to be addressed, she was tired of talking about cars and money on today of all days. 'Are you going to the cemetery?'

'Cemetery?'

She heard the bemusement in her brother's voice and anger burnt inside her as she responded. 'It's their one-year anniversary, Mark.'

'I know.'

Natasha was quite sure he'd forgotten. 'Well?' she pushed. 'Are you going?'

As he reeled off yet more excuses Natasha simply hung up the phone and headed to her bedroom. But instead of getting on with tidying up, for a moment or two she sat on her bed, wondering how everything could have gone so wrong. This time last year her life had been pretty close to perfect—she'd just qualified as a teacher and had been doing a job she loved; she had been dating a guy she was starting to if not love then really care for; she'd been saving towards moving out of her parents' house. She had also been looking forward to being a bridesmaid at her brother's wedding.

Now, in the space of a year, all she had known, all she had loved, had been taken. Even her job. As an infant school teacher she had been on a temporary placement and about to be offered a permanent position when the car crash had happened. Knowing she simply couldn't be the teacher she wanted to be while deeply grieving, she had declined the job offer, and the last year had been filled with temporary placements as she waded through her parents' estate.

Their will had been very specific—the family home was to be sold and the profits divided equally between their two children.

How she had hated that—how much harder it had made things having to deal with estate agents and home inspections.

And going through all the contents had been agony. It was a job she felt should have been done in stages; she had wanted to linger more in the process of letting go. But Mark had wanted his share and had pushed things along. Her boyfriend, Jason, had been no help either. He'd been uncomfortable with her grief and uncomfortable providing comfort—it had been a relief for Natasha to end things.

And now, one year on, she sat in the small home she had bought that still felt unfamiliar, living a life that didn't feel like her own.

Tears wouldn't change anything; sitting on her bed crying wasn't going to help. She headed downstairs and, one cup of coffee later, unable to face a bus, she called for a taxi, asking him to stop and wait as she went into a florist and bought some flowers.

She hated coming here.

Wasn't it supposed to bring her peace?

It didn't.

She looked at the headstone and all Natasha felt was anger that her parents had been taken far too soon.

'Maybe it's too soon for peace?' Natasha said aloud to them, except her heart craved it.

No, there was no peace to be had at the cemetery, so she took a bus home and had a long bath to warm up.

Anticipating packing for her holiday, Natasha had pulled out all her clothes, and late that afternoon she tackled the mountain strewn over her bedroom. But Rakhal and their brief encounter was still there at the back of her mind, and he was so much nicer to think about than her problems closer to home that she allowed herself a tiny dream...

What if she *had* said yes to him?

What, Natasha wondered, did you wear for dinner with the Crown Prince Sheikh of Alzirz?

Nothing that was in Natasha's wardrobe, that was for sure. Except as she hung up her clothes there it was—still wrapped in its cover. She had never really known what to do with it. It was to have been her bridesmaid's dress for Mark and Louise's wedding, but Louise had called the wedding off a week before the date, which had left

Mark devastated. It was then he had started gambling—or rather that was what he had told Natasha when he'd come to her for help. Now she wondered if it had been the reason for Louise calling things off.

She had been so angry with Louise for destroying her brother. The car accident resulting in the death of their parents had been devastating, but the upcoming wedding, though hard to look forward to at first, had been the one shining light—Mark and Louise had been together for years, and her calling it off had had the most terrible effect on Mark.

Yet now Natasha was starting to wonder if Mark had been the one who had destroyed himself—if his gambling problems were in fact not so recent.

She hadn't spoken with Louise since the break-up. Louise had always been lovely, and for the first time Natasha allowed herself to miss her almost-sister-in-law. She resisted the urge to call her, because Louise didn't need to be worried with Mark's problems now.

Instead, Natasha slid open the zip and

pulled the dress from its cover. As she gazed at it she wished again that things had turned out differently.

It was gold and very simple, with a slightly fluted hem that was cut on the bias, and thin spaghetti straps that fell into a cowl neck. It would be wrong to pull it on with wet hair and an unmade-up face, for if ever there was a dress that deserved the full effect it was this one.

So Natasha dried hair and then smoothed it with straighteners. Louise had wanted her to wear her hair up. It was the only thing they had disagreed on, but of course it was to have been Louise's day, and so she would have won. Natasha took her thick red hair and twisted it, securing it on the top of the head with a clasp, then put on make-up as best she could. She took out her mother's earrings and necklace, holding the cool pearls in her hand for a moment. Natasha rarely wore jewellery for the same reason she didn't wear perfume: it irritated her skin. But today she made an exception and put the jewels on. It should still be her mother wearing them. How Natasha wished that she could rewind a year, because things had been so much simpler then.

But if she started crying she might never stop, so Natasha looked in the mirror instead. The dress was stunning and Louise had been right—with her hair up it was even more so. The necklace and earrings were the perfect final touch and, again as Louise had assured her, she didn't look like a traditional bridesmaid. More…Natasha looked again and gave a smile. Had she said yes to Rakhal, this was what she would have worn, for now she was fit for a prince.

Still he played on her mind—but then why wouldn't he? He had been the one saving grace in a pretty miserable day. And then she heard a knock at her door.

Perhaps it was Mark bringing over the money? Or an aunt dropping round to mark the one-year anniversary of her parents' passing?

While normally she would have run down the stairs to answer, given how she was dressed Natasha held back and went to the window. She peeked through a gap in the curtain. Peering down into the street, she saw a limousine—but even before that she knew it was him.

Had known at some level that she had been dressing for him.

That this morning their attraction, or whatever it was that had occurred, hadn't all been in her imagination, that he had felt it too.

And now Rakhal was at her door.

CHAPTER TWO

RAKHAL had spent the day trying to forget Natasha. He had completed the most pressing of his appointments and then peered through the impressive list of female contacts in his phone.

This evening none of them had appealed.

He could, if he'd chosen to, have returned to the exclusive London club he often frequented, where he was assured of a warm welcome from any number of young socialites who would be only too happy to spend a night in a prince's bed.

He'd chosen not to.

Instead he had headed down to the hotel bar, taken a seat in a plump leather chair. In a moment a long glass of water had been placed in front of him, for here in London, it was his drink of choice. Less than two

minutes later, another option had appeared.
Blonde, beautiful, her smile inviting.

With but a gesture of his hand he could
have invited her to join him or have a drink
sent over to her.

It was that easy for Rakhal.

Always.

Both here and at home.

He'd thought of the harem that served
his every need—the harem that would still
serve him even after his marriage—and
suddenly he'd been weary with *easy*. He
was bored with no thrill to the chase.

He'd gestured to the bartender, who had
walked over ready to take his order, to
serve the blonde a glass of champagne, but
Rakhal had delivered other instructions.

Now the car he had summoned waited
as he knocked again at her door. Rakhal
did not have time to play games, and neither did he have time to take his time. And
yet here he was. All day she had intrigued
him. All day his first taste of rejection had
gnawed. Perhaps she was already in a relationship? he had pondered. But something
told him she was not. There was a shyness
to her, an awkwardness he found endear-

ing. Rarely was effort required from him with women—perhaps that was the novelty that had brought him here.

He decided that the novelty would quickly wane, but that thought faded as soon as she opened the door.

It was as though she'd been waiting for him—had somehow anticipated his surprise arrival.

Appealing before, she was exquisite now. Her hair was dry, its true colours revealed: the colours of a winter sky in Alzirz as the sun dipped lower over the desert, reds and oranges and a blaze of fire. His only qualm was that he wanted to see it worn down— *would* see it worn down, Rakhal decided, before the night's end.

'What are you doing here?' Natasha had had her panic upstairs and was as calm as she could manage now—as casual as she could hope to be when dealing with the sudden arrival of Rakhal.

'I said that I would pick you up at seven.'

'And I told you I had plans…' Natasha started. Yet she did want time with this intoxicating man and her refusal was halted. For all day she had regretted saying no to him, all day she had wished she had said yes, and now she had her chance. 'Actually, my plans have changed…' She hoped her make-up hid her blush as she lied. 'My friend isn't feeling well.'

'Well, now that your plans have changed…' He knew she was lying, and he would not ask her to join him again. He had asked her once, had even come to her door. Now he stood silently awaiting her decision, for it was up to Natasha now—he did not beg.

The decision was an easy one. He was even more beautiful than she remembered him from this morning. He was wearing an immaculate charcoal-grey suit and his hair, messy that morning, was now swept back. The bruise on his eye had turned a deep purple, and Natasha felt her nails dig into her palms as she resisted the urge to reach out and touch it, to run her fingers over the slight swelling at his left cheekbone. It was bizarre the effect he had on her. Never had a man made her more aware of her femininity.

Natasha swallowed, for he made her aware of her sexuality too, in a way no one ever had—certainly not Jason. She was filled with a sudden desperation for the night not to end—and it would, Natasha knew, if she did not go with him now. It would end this instant if she did not simply say yes.

'I'll get my bag.' Natasha hovered a moment, unsure if she should ask him in—embarrassed to do so, but worried it would be rude not to. 'Do you want to—?'

'I will wait here,' Rakhal interrupted. He wanted their night to start, and was not sure if she lived alone. If she did—well, he did not want to ruin any tentative progress with a kiss delivered too soon. It would be hard not to kiss her. He was already growing hard.

He turned out to face the street, to look at the neat hedges and the houses. He tried to fathom her, tried to work her out just a little, surprising himself because for once he had a need to know more about the woman he would be spending the night with.

She found a bag and quickly filled it with her purse and keys, then took a moment more to steady herself than to check her make-up. She found a jacket that didn't really do justice to the dress. Even though it had stopped raining it was a cold, clear night, and she really couldn't go out with bare arms, so she slipped it on and walked down the stairs. She could see his outline in the front doorway as he waited for her to be ready.

He waited too while she locked the door, and then they headed to his car. This time it was his driver who came around and opened the door, and there was no man in robes waiting inside when she climbed in. She was nervous at being alone with him.

Yet he was the perfect gentleman. He took the seat opposite rather than next to her, making polite conversation as the car moved through the dark streets. He did nothing and said nothing untoward—in fact he didn't even comment on how she was dressed. No doubt he was used to going out with women dressed up to the nines. She wondered how he'd have reacted if he knew just how unusual this was for her, if she'd answered the door in jeans and slippers. Would the outcome have been the same? Would he have waited while she changed…? Would the usual outfits in her wardrobe have sufficed for a night like this?

She doubted it.

Yet he had seen her dripping wet this morning, had seen her at her worst, and still there had been *want* between them. The doubt blurred as she pondered this most stunning man. She could see his hand resting on his thigh, the dark skin, the manicured nails, and then she turned her gaze away when she realised he was watching her too. Her jacket felt like a blanket. The car was too warm. Both these things she blamed for the heat that spread across her body as she admitted her desire. She wanted to press a button, wanted the window to open and the night air to blast her face cool. When they turned a corner and his stretched-out leg rolled just a little nearer to her rigid feet she wanted to lift her feet to his waiting hands, to simply be ravished.

They pulled up outside a luxurious hotel. As the door opened Natasha saw faces turning and was uncomfortable with this rare scrutiny from onlookers. She was grateful when his hand took her arm, and told herself that it was Rakhal they were looking at as they were welcomed and then led through the hotel and into a restaurant.

Again he turned heads.

Natasha knew it had nothing to do with *her*, for the place was filled with jewelled and made-up women. It was Rakhal who drew the eye, Rakhal who had forks pausing on their way to ruby-red mouths and small murmurs rippling across tables as people attempted to place him. And no wonder, Natasha thought as she took a seat, with his dark looks, his elegance, there was a poise to him that could never truly be taught.

And tonight *she* was dining with him.

The table was beautifully set with white tablecloths and candles, and the silverware and glasses gleamed, yet it was not the luxurious surroundings that unnerved her, but the company that she kept. It wasn't his title that intimidated either—well, perhaps a bit, Natasha conceded—but really it was the man himself that had her stomach folding over on itself, had her still unsure as to whether she should have said yes to his offer. Because despite the silk of his manners there was that edge to him. She knew she had taken on more than she could ever handle.

The waiters lavished attention on them, pulling out chairs and spreading napkins over their laps as Rakhal ordered champagne.

Natasha declined. 'Not for me, thank you. I'd prefer to drink water.' Oh, she knew the cost of a bottle of champagne would be nothing to him, but somehow she didn't want to feel beholden, and she was also mindful that her common sense was somewhat lacking around him. Champagne might only exacerbate the fact.

Rakhal too, it seemed, was only drinking water, for he cancelled the champagne, ordered iced water and then turned his attention to Natasha. 'Is there anything you are allergic to?' he asked. 'Or anything you particularly do not like to eat?'

'Oh!' It was a rather unusual question. 'I'll just wait to have a look at the menu, thank you.'

'I will make the selections,' Rakhal responded.

Natasha felt her lips tighten. She certainly did not want him choosing her dinner for her, and she told him the same. 'I'd like to wait and see the menu.'

She was determined to win on this—for this was a man who didn't usually take no for an answer. Not this morning when she had declined his lift, nor tonight when he had come to her door despite her turning down his invitation to dinner. And now he thought he could choose what she ate. Well, he had chosen the wrong person if that was the case.

Her voice held a warning when she spoke again. 'I can order for myself, thank you!'

'I'm sure you can. But I have asked my chef to prepare a banquet, so he needs to know if there are foods to which you are averse.'

'Your chef?'

'I stay regularly at this hotel and so I ensure there is a chef from Alzirz. Naturally when I'm away the other guests get to sample his delightful cooking, but tonight he is preparing food exclusively for us...' He watched the movement in her throat as she swallowed. 'Of course I can have him come out and discuss your preferences, if you'd prefer…?'

'No.' Natasha shook her head, her face flushed, more than a little embarrassed at the fuss she had made. 'That won't be necessary.'

And Rakhal watched her blush, visible even in candlelight. 'Perhaps I could have somebody write down the ingredients so you can check through them…' He was enjoying this now.

'Of course not. I'm sure it will be lovely. It is more that I thought you were choosing *for* me…'

'I am,' Rakhal said, and watched her rapid blinking. 'Tonight you are my guest, and you should not be worrying about making decisions. Say I were to come to your house tomorrow for dinner…' He watched the red darken on her cheeks as she pictured it. 'Perhaps you would ask my preferences, but you would not give me a menu.' He leaned forward a little. 'You would prepare dishes that you thought might please your guest. Well, I do not cook, but I have asked my chef to do the same…to cook with foods that are fresh and flown in from my country.'

'You have food flown in?' How spoilt *was* this man? she wondered, taking a sip of her drink.

'And water too...' Rakhal responded without a qualm. 'I am served water that is sourced from my home.'

She paused as she raised the glass to her lips. French champagne probably cost less. And then, as he had since the moment they met, he surprised her again.

'If I am to give wise counsel then I should be nourished by my land...'

A waiter topped up her glass as the first course was brought: a selection of dips and breads and fruits. Rakhal explained his selections.

'The water is from a spring deep in the desert, and this is what I always start with.' He picked up a date and a small silver knife. 'Usually they are served quartered, but I prefer to pit my own.'

He slid the knife through the shiny fruit and exposed the stone. She felt her stomach curl as he inverted the date and popped the stone out. How, Natasha tried to fathom, could slicing a date be seductive?

Dates were something her grandmother served at Christmas.

Dates were prunes.

Dates were not sexy.

He dipped it in some oily goo and she watched his long slender fingers swirl it around. Then he lifted it to her mouth and she accepted, trying to touch only the fruit. But her lips met his fingers and she had to force her mouth not to linger, to take the fruit, not to capture his hand and taste his fingers. It scared her, the effect he had on her, the places he took her mind to. And she knew that he knew it as he pulled his hand away.

As Natasha chewed the rich fruit, she amended her thoughts.

Dates *were* sexy.

'It is called *haysa al tumreya.*'

His voice was low and for her ears only, and she tasted the hot sauce around the sweet date as she listened.

'The date tree is the most important. It provides shade around the spring...'

As they ate he told her about the oasis in

the desert, about the fruits and ripe peaches for nectar and about the aubergines that made the *baba ganoush* she tried next. It held a smoky flavour that had her closing her eyes in bliss as she tasted it. He told her about the foods that grew beneath the tall date trees, and she ate and she listened and she looked, and he was intriguing rather than spoilt, and at each turn more beautiful still.

Rakhal was right. It was nice to be spoiled, not to have to make any decisions, simply to listen and to talk as they shared the sumptuous food. He told her a little about his land, about his life in Alzirz, and she told him a little about herself too—or rather he asked her about her family.

'My parents were killed last year in a motor accident,' Natasha said. She waited for the flurry of sympathy, but he simply stared and waited for her to go on. 'I have an older brother. Mark.'

'And he takes care of you?'

'I take care of *myself*,' Natasha answered. Aware her response might have been a little brittle, she softened it. 'It's been a difficult year, but I manage.'

She was relieved when they were disturbed by the waiters bringing another impressive course, and then he told her more about the land from which he came. About the palace that looked out to the ocean and the desert abode to which he escaped.

'It sounds beautiful.'

'You would love it,' Rakhal assured her, and for a moment he glimpsed her there— the jewel in his harem.

They ate more food from his country, and she could taste the sun. When he could not hear something she said he moved his chair around the table until he sat next to her. Dessert was a shared plate, and he fed her fruit from his fingers again. Sometimes Natasha forgot she was in a busy restaurant. Sometimes she forgot her own inexperience under the gaze of this very experienced man. For his voice made her ears ache to hear him, had her inching a little closer to him.

For Rakhal too this night was different. There was candour—he normally would not tell a woman such things about his home, about his life and his thoughts, but with her conversation was pleasing. Now they were speaking of traditions, and he was honest—telling her that one day he would marry, that he would return to Alzirz and select his bride. Though he was not completely honest, for he did not tell her it would be soon.

'How do you choose?' She was more than a little curious. 'Will she be wealthy? From another royal family, perhaps?'

'We do not need wealth—Alzirz is rare in that its royals choose their partners from the people. My grandmother was Sheikha Queen; my grandfather was a wise man from the desert. She chose him for his knowledge, for at times the country moves too quickly and we need to remember the ways and teachings of old. When I am King...'

'You will be *King*!' Natasha couldn't keep the surprise from her voice. 'Are you scared?'

He gave her an extremely quizzical look. 'I am never scared.'

She doubted he was. She had never met a man so assured. 'So you're the eldest?'

'I have no brothers or sisters.' He saw her slight frown and it was merited—because in his country it was expected that there would be many heirs. It was imperative to the country's survival, in fact. 'My mother died giving birth.'

'I'm sorry.'

Rakhal did not do sentiment. He had been brought up without it and, as his father had explained, he could not miss someone he had never known. But there was a twist somewhere inside him as she expressed her condolences.

'What was she like?'

'She died giving birth to me,' Rakhal said again. 'How would I know?'

It was certainly rarely discussed. In fact Rakhal could only recall a few brief conversations where his mother had been mentioned even in passing. Needing more, he had once spoken with an old man in the desert—a man who, it was rumoured, had lived for one hundred and twenty yellow moons. But tonight was the first time someone had directly asked him about his mother.

'You must know *something*?'

'She was from the desert too,' Rakhal said. 'From an ancient tribe with rare lineage.' He remembered what the old man had told him. 'She was apparently a wise and beautiful soul.'

He had revealed too much—or rather more than he was used to. He looked down and saw their hands intertwined. Rakhal was not usually a man who held hands, not in this way, and so he reverted to ways more usual for him to get the night back to where he felt safer. He pressed his thumb into her palm. The beat of pressure and the slide of his fingers around her wrist had the colour rising on her cheeks. He was tired of talking. He wanted to bed her. But when she did not return the pressure, when she rather pointedly removed her hand from his, Rakhal made no attempt to retrieve it.

'I should take you home.'

He should, for the restaurant was practically empty. And yet she was curiously disappointed and terribly conflicted as he led her through the foyer. He'd been the perfect gentleman—only she wasn't sure it was a perfect gentleman she wanted. But their night was coming to its conclusion, for she would not be asking him in.

And perhaps Rakhal realised that. Re-

alised that this might be his last chance.
For he halted her, turned her to face him.

'Have you enjoyed this evening?'

'Very much.'

'I have enjoyed talking with you.'

She did not understand how rare, how
unique this compliment was—could not
understand that Rakhal did not do deep
conversations with the women he dated.
And yet he had enjoyed talking with Natasha.

He smiled to himself as the colour rose
from her neck to her ears. He saw the pearls
that hung from her earlobes and his fingers
moved and captured one.

'These are beautiful.'

'They were my mother's. I don't usually wear jewellery...' She moved her head
away from him—just a little, but enough
to signal a warning. A warning Rakhal did
not heed. Instead his other hand moved to
the jewel that hung on her chest, a heavier
pearl, and he recognised its beauty. He was
surrounded by it after all.

'Why not?'

'I don't like it...' She could hardly get the
words out, could not carry on a conversa-

tion with his hands so close, with his fingers grazing her flesh. 'It irritates…' she attempted. But it didn't tonight, and neither did the fingers near her throat. Her skin almost begged for more of him. 'But I make an exception sometimes for these.'

'I can see why. The pearls are exquisite.'

She could hardly breathe. One hand was at her ear, the other near her throat, and she felt trapped, cornered—but deliciously so.

'They were actually my grandmother's…' Her voice was too high and breathy. She was sure he did not want her family history—except these were the one precious thing that remained. Oh, they weren't worth a fortune, but the antique rose-gold was precious, and there was just so much history there. 'And her mother's before that. She…'

Rakhal picked up a strand of red hair that had escaped from the clasp and ran it through his fingers, then brushed it behind her ear, his fingers trailing along her neck. His knowing eyes watched the pulse quicken. Feeling the beat of it on his warm fingers, he wanted her hair down. He wanted to taste her mouth and he wanted it *now*.

Perhaps he knew how his kiss would affect her. For before it was delivered he moved her to a wall, to a darkened alcove away from other guests and the night concierge, to a place where she was almost alone with him. And there was so much want in his dark eyes, so much sex in his gaze, it frightened her more than he could know.

'Perhaps I should…' Natasha had started to tell him she should perhaps get home, because now the moment had arrived she was both wanting and terrified, but then she could not speak for his mouth was on hers.

He had chosen his moment carefully, in the midst of a sentence, when her mind was just a touch less on him. He tasted first lipstick, and he saw her eyes widen, and then he did not look any more. He closed his eyes and felt instead—felt her momentary resistance, a brief flailing in his arms and then acceptance.

And she did accept—for how nice it was to kiss him, or rather to be kissed by such a man. Nothing came close, for when his mouth found hers quite simply it overruled.

It overruled fear, it overruled logic, it blew out logical thought processes—all it did was consume. All night she had wondered about this moment, when the skilled attack might come, and even with him so close, still when the moment had arrived it had surprised her. And the kiss surprised her too, for it surpassed all she had known, all she'd thought she knew, all she'd even dreamed. His lips were soft, yet firm, and extremely insistent. His hands were precise. They went to her shoulders and kept her still as he kissed her thoroughly, as he drowned that first futile hint of protest with his mouth, and she felt the muscle of his tongue and flared at the taste of him.

Completely instant was her response, and there, beneath the layer of cologne that had teased her since the morning, was a musky male scent that was simply a trigger, for her hands shot to his hair and her fingers knotted into the silken raven locks. It revealed more than teasing for her senses, for his hair was glossy with exotic pomade, and she inhaled the oils. Her mouth moved to his command, and when it did, when she was gone, when he knew she was ready, he toppled her a little more against him, moved her deeper into his embrace.

It was more instinct than a plan he was following now. For Rakhal, too, this kiss was different. It was a kiss that was not just about what was to follow.

Rarely did he fully indulge—when he returned to Alzirz, in the time before he chose his wife, every need of his would be met by his harem. There would be no need to kiss, no need to arouse. It would be *his* pleasure that was the mutual goal. And then he would marry—and, yes, he would kiss and arouse his wife, but with a different aim. For she would be removed from his bed after two days. And as he waited for news of a successful coupling his harem would indulge him again.

But here in this strange country there were different rules: women's demands were different. It was a place where you kissed for pleasure.

What a pleasure.

His tongue was probing, his chin rough, his mouth smooth, and his hands knowing—reading her want as if it were dotted in Braille on her dress. They were down at her waist and then at her hips, pulling her in a little more, enough for her to feel his hardness. She gasped into his mouth and forgot her surroundings, arched into him. He pressed her in still further and she felt him through her clothes, felt a rare wild recklessness—*that* was what he made her feel—that a man she had met just this morning could have her cast her morals to the wind.

He would never know the struggle as she forced her body to halt.

He felt her lips pull away and could only admire her, for there was heat beneath his fingers and her breath was rapid and soft on his cheek, her eyes dilated with arousal. Another moment, Rakhal was sure, she'd have come—and not just to his room.

'I will get you home.'

She was shaking beneath his fingers and he must not rush her. She was a virgin, Rakhal was quite sure of it—which was an incredibly rare treat these days.

Tomorrow, Rakhal vowed.

On his last night as a single man in London he would bed her.

Rakhal was completely certain.

CHAPTER THREE

THE ride home was not what she was expecting.

Natasha had thought, as she stepped into the limousine, that she would spend the journey fending him off—especially when this time he sat next to her. She had, after all, felt his fierce erection, had tasted the passion of his kiss. Her lips still felt bruised and swollen, and her body could not settle.

His thigh sometimes met hers as the vehicle turned a corner, but there was no repeat of the kiss, and, unlike Natasha, Rakhal seemed completely calm, perhaps even a little indifferent. She wondered if he was annoyed—if perhaps he thought she had led him on… She wasn't even sure, as they pulled up at her house, if she would see him again—but so badly she wanted to.

He did not attempt to reclaim her mouth.

Just gave her a brief kiss on the cheek as the driver came round to get the door. Nor did he try to angle for an invitation to come in.

He wished her goodnight and saw the flicker of confusion in her eyes as the car door was opened and cold air climbed in. Rakhal knew exactly what he was doing. Tonight she would lie burning, recalling their kiss, wondering if he would call her, and he would keep her wondering—would time things carefully. When she was sure she had blown it, when she was sure it was over, her doorbell would ring and there would be flowers and jewels to soothe her, and…

Rakhal watched her climb out of the car, saw the feminine curves that tomorrow he would caress, and for the second time in his life thought he would enjoy choosing a gift. He had kissed her as she wore gold and he would take her when she wore silver. A dress would be included in his gift…

Not that Natasha knew that.

She should be relieved, she told herself. She had had the most wonderful night, Rakhal had been a wonderful companion, not quite the perfect gentleman, and yet she was disappointed. Her body still twitched from his touch; her heart still skipped as she reached her door.

She turned around and gave a brief wave. She certainly would not ask him in to her modest house. But as she went to push in the key she frowned as the door opened under the weight of her hand alone and she saw that the lock was broken.

The driver awaited Rakhal's instruction, and Rakhal waited for her to step inside. He frowned as she turned to him. Her eyes were urgent and he could see the fear on her face. Immediately he stepped from the car.

She didn't need to say it. One look into the hall and it was clear she had been burgled.

He walked past her, went straight inside, and saw that it was in chaos. Drawers had been pulled out, and the sofa had been slashed. He halted Natasha as she went to run upstairs, caught her wrist and pulled her down to his level.

'I will check upstairs,' Rakhal said, in-

stantly taking control. 'You will wait in
my car.'

He was relieved that he had not driven
off sooner, worried too as to what might
have happened if he had not taken her out
that night. He went to climb the stairs and
check for himself if the intruder was still
there. Rakhal had no fear, his irritation was
only that she did not obey him—for as he
reached the top of the stairs Natasha came
up behind him.

'Go back down,' he ordered. 'I told you
to wait in the car.'

But she brushed past him, opening her
bedroom door, and he heard her sob of
horror. He was black with fury. The mat-
tress was slashed too, the wardrobe emp-
tied, boxes, bags—everything lay strewn
and torn.

'You are to go down and wait in the car.'
His driver had come into the house now,
and he was almost as dark and as forbidding as his master. Rakhal spoke to him in
Arabic. 'Go with him,' Rakhal said. 'You
are safe. I will call the police…'

'Please don't.' They were the first words
she had spoken since leaving the car and

he could hear the shock and terror in her voice. 'Please, Rakhal, I don't want you to call the police.'

'Of course I must. You must report this...'

'No!'

She'd held onto her tears for so long, scared of what she might unleash, and she held them back now. She pressed her fingers into her eyes to stop them from falling, clamped her mouth on her chattering teeth and swallowed the scream that was building.

She managed words instead, scarcely able to believe what she was saying, yet knowing in her heart that it was true. 'I think that's exactly what my brother wants me to do.'

She was incredibly grateful that Rakhal was here, that he did not ask questions, that he did not pry. Instead he held her for a moment and then led her to his car. He poured something into a small glass and then added water and ice. She watched the fluid turn milky. This time it was not tea.

'Arak,' he informed her, and she took a sip.

It was strong and sickly and she tasted

anise. It burnt as it made its way down to her stomach. She sipped slowly as he made a few phone calls—though not to the police, for he spoke in his own language.

'I have people coming to the house to make sure it is safe.' He looked at her. 'Are you sure you do not want me to call the police?'

'I don't think I'll be calling to report the robbery,' Natasha said.

'You really believe that your brother would do this to you?'

'I don't know what to think at the moment,' Natasha admitted. 'But if it was him I'm not sure I'm ready to turn in my own brother.' Panic was rising within her. Maybe she was wrong. Maybe it was a simple burglary. 'I don't know what to do—'

'I told you earlier,' Rakhal interrupted, 'you do not have to make any decisions tonight.' There was no question of him leaving her here to deal with this alone. 'You will come back to my hotel with me.'

CHAPTER FOUR

'EVERYTHING is being taken care of.'

They were back at the hotel, in his sumptuous suite, though Natasha didn't really take in her surroundings. She sat on a chair as he made another phone call, and despite the warmth of the room she felt as cold as if she was sitting out in the street. It wasn't so much the burglary that had upset her, more the thought that Mark could stoop so low. She knew that now she was safe, and that now that things were being dealt with, Rakhal would have some questions, but when he came off the phone he told her first what he had done.

'I have a member of my staff at your home,' Rakhal explained. 'I have informed him that he is not to touch anything—that will give you some time to decide how you want to proceed. Now, I must ask you again—do you really think your brother did this?'

'Yes.' It was the most terrible admission, it actually hurt to say it, but she was tired of covering up for Mark and exhausted from the stress.

'Why would he terrify you like this?'

'Money.' Natasha's eyes briefly met Rakhal's, but then she tore her gaze away, guilty at her admission, as if she were betraying Mark by voicing it. She still hoped that she was wrong. 'I'm going to ring him…'

'And say what?'

'I don't know,' Natasha admitted. 'Maybe I'm wrong…' Her heart lurched with hope she knew was false. 'Maybe I've just been incredibly unlucky to have my car stolen and my house broken into on the same day…' Then she closed her eyes, remembering what her brother had said about the car insurance.

'I will give you some privacy,' Rakhal said, and she was grateful for that.

She spoke with Mark for perhaps a minute at best, and then sat for a moment or two more in silence, till Rakhal came out. She gave him a pale smile.

'I'm not unlucky.'

'I'm sorry.'

So too was Natasha—more than he could know.

'Did he admit to it?' Rakhal asked.

'Of course not,' Natasha said. 'And he doesn't even suspect that I think it's him—I just knew from his voice, from the questions he asked…'

'Natasha, can you tell me what is going on?'

'It's not your concern.' She really hadn't told anybody. Oh, her friends knew in part, but she had never really revealed all of it to anyone. 'It's better that you don't get involved.'

'I became involved when you asked that I do not call the police,' Rakhal said, and then he looked at her pale features, and the unshed tears in her eyes, and in an unguarded moment he spoke from his heart. 'And you are my concern.'

She was.

Whatever had taken place today would not end as he had first planned. He knew

that this was more than one of his regular
one-night stands—knew that even when he
flew to the desert on Monday, even when
he married, still she would be on his mind.

Still he would take care of her.

'It's complicated,' Natasha said.

Rakhal doubted that it was, but he said
nothing. Instead he let her talk.

'My brother was supposed to get married six months ago.' She hated talking
about family things—her parents had always been so private and she was too. You
dealt with things without asking for help;
that was the way she had been brought up.
Yet her brother didn't seem to have inher-
ited the same resilience. 'A week before the
wedding his fiancée, Louise, called it off.'

Still Rakhal said nothing, simply let her
speak.

'Since then he's been going off the
rails. When my parents died the family
home was sold…that's when I bought my
house—well, some of it. I have a mort-
gage…' Natasha said, uncomfortable discussing money with a man who clearly had
so much of it. She was worried that he'd
think she was asking for his help.

But he gave her a nod, told her to go on. And she wasn't exactly volunteering the information—his silence was dragging it out of her.

'But after he and Louise broke up Mark just burnt his money.'

'Burnt?' Rakhal frowned.

'Not literally,' she answered. 'He started gambling, bought a flash car… He owes a lot of people money. A couple of months ago I took out a loan for him. I was able to get one because I had the house…'

'Is he repaying the loan?'

'He was—but not this month.'

'One moment.' His phone was ringing. He glanced at it before answering, then took the call.

Natasha sat there as he spoke in his language, and it gave her a pause. She was embarrassed and angry that her one perfect night had turned out like this—that yet again Mark had spectacularly ruined things. She was embarrassed, too, at all she had told Rakhal, and Natasha wanted out.

'Where are you going?'

'Home,' Natasha said. 'Look, thank you

for a lovely evening. I really am sorry about how it turned out.'

'You're not going home.'

She gave a tight smile—she certainly didn't need this.

'I'll be fine…'

'Natasha, that call was from my aide. Your brother has just gone to your home. It would seem he is a very angry man. He's looking for some jewels. He says that they are his…'

She knew that that was what he had been looking for—the pearls she was wearing tonight—that Mark would insist she put them down as stolen on her insurance claim and, worse than that, in her heart she knew that had she not been wearing them he would have sold them. He would have sold them and then had her claim the insurance money. She was simply too drained to cry, too exhausted to think.

'You must rest,' Rakhal said. 'I will ring and book you a suite.'

'I don't need a suite,' Natasha said. 'The sofa will be fine.'

'My guests do not sleep on a sofa.' He was in no mood to argue, and neither was he that much of a gentleman. 'And neither do I.'

'Please, don't…' She ran a worried hand over her forehead. It seemed stupid but she did not want to be alone—and if that was the price… She recalled his kiss, the bliss she had found in his arms, and knew it was a price she was only too willing to pay.

But Rakhal did not like to win by default. And then he saw her jump as her phone rang, saw tension tighten her features as she took the call.

'That's not your concern, Mark.' She screwed her eyes closed. 'There isn't much missing… *I'll* decide if I speak to the police.'

'Turn off the phone,' Rakhal instructed. He was worried for her. Her brother was out of control now that his plan was not working. 'You did not tell him where you are?' Rakhal checked.

'I just told him I had booked into a hotel. He'd never guess it's this one…'

Rakhal wasn't taking any chances. 'You will stay here tonight.' There was another bedroom in his luxurious suite and he showed it to her. 'A bath has been run for

me but you are to take it. You need some
time to wind down. I will have a shower
first…'

Natasha sat in the lounge as he show-
ered, touched that he had not pressed her
in any way, had not taken her in his arms
to comfort her, for she knew very well how
it could have turned out. She was terribly
glad that he had been there—tried not to
picture how tonight might have been had
she not met Rakhal.

'I am done.'

He walked into the lounge, a white towel
around his hips, and she saw the snake of
hair she had glimpsed that morning, the
bruises on his shoulder from his battle
with the police and the aggrieved husband.
His skin was wet, his hair was too, and in
the middle of one of the worst nights she
glimpsed the possibility of the best night of
her life. Her throat was tight as she looked
at him and, though touched at his thought-
fulness, that he had not pressed, a part of
her rued it too.

'I am going to bed,' Rakhal said, for he
could feel the change in her tension, could
see the need for escape in her eyes, and

he too was remembering their kiss. But he would keep his word to himself. 'You take your time. Tonight this is your home.'

She let out a breath as he closed the bedroom door, then headed to the bathroom and undressed. She should be in tears, or scared or something, but she looked in the mirror and saw lust in her eyes, and she was so very aware that he was near.

Natasha had thought that, given it had been run a while ago, the bath would be cool when finally she stepped into it, but of course it was scented and warm, for she was in *his* world now…and she wanted his bed.

Rakhal wanted her too. He lay awake and tried not to think of her bathing. There was no question of sleeping. He was more than used to a woman in his suite—just not in the spare room. He listened to the gurgle as the water drained, and tried and failed not to picture her climbing out. He was hard beneath the sheet but he resisted, lay there liking the rare feeling of unsated arousal, savouring his restraint, anticipating the reward—because tomorrow he knew she'd be his.

He did not regret his earlier choice of words to her.

She *was* his concern now.

Except on Monday he must return to his land and time was fast running out. He thought of the harem, but perhaps she would not be receptive to that suggestion, and he thought too about keeping her as a mistress in London. It was an intensely pleasurable thought; he would grant her the gold stamp in her passport that would give her full privileges, would enable her to visit him freely. When he heard her pad past his door he had to bite on his lip so as not to summon her in and share the news.

He had promised himself tomorrow.

A prince did not break a vow.

CHAPTER FIVE

NATASHA was awoken by the sound of silence—only then did she realise the full extent of the usual background noise of a hotel. The heating whirred and then stilled; the alarm clock stopped ticking; the darkness blackened further. Natasha sat up, taking a moment to remember where she was and all that had happened. She tried the light at her bedside but it wasn't working, and then patted the end of the bed. She found the thick bathrobe, still damp from her bathing. Pulling it on, she made her way out of bed, her hands in front of her to find the window, but even as she parted the blinds there was nothing to see: the streetlights and neon signs were all out.

'It's a power cut.' Rakhal had been awake anyway, and he spoke as soon as she opened her bedroom door. 'The back-up generator should kick in soon...'

It was darker than she had ever known it, and she was grateful when he crossed the room. Then she felt awkward as she put her hand up to him and encountered skin.

'Sorry.' Even though it begged to linger she pulled her hand away, and despite the dark she was sure he was smiling at her nervousness.

But Rakhal was not smiling. His eyes were long accustomed to the dark and he could see the parting of her lips. He was resisting the urge to kiss her, for all night the kiss they had shared had been driving him wild.

He could smell her, and it was different—for the bath had been prepared for *him*, and her feminine scent now mingled with the exotic oils of the desert. He wanted to take her, wanted to stay in the darkness and simply give in. And he could, Rakhal realised, for it was tomorrow now—midnight had long since gone. So he lowered his head and brushed her lips. She jerked her head just a bit, and then he found her mouth again.

Just a dust of his lips was all he gave her, and then again, and then once more. It was a different kiss, a tease of a kiss, because this time it was Rakhal who pulled his lips back just a little, till her hungry mouth searched for his.

And still his mouth stayed gentle. It was Natasha's lips that were insistent. But he did not return the pressure till her mouth was almost begging, raining kisses on lips that stayed loose, and then he relented, gave her the bliss of his tongue and a mouth that was slow and measured. He made sure she was frantic for his soothing and then, without warning, without even subtly checking, his hand slipped into her dressing gown and caressed a nipple that was hard and waiting. He slid his palm over the soft skin till it was essential that his other hand held her or she might sink to the floor.

But he did not hold her.

He let her become dizzy and weak, he let his towel fall, and she let her robe open so his manhood rested on her stomach. Her lips were on his shoulder now, she was leaning on him as if to regroup, but he did not let her; he kissed her ear to blot out the whispers of doubt that chained her and licked at the tender flesh beneath her lobe till she moaned on his shoulder. Her hand moved to explore what would soon be inside her. He kissed her neck and tasted the pearls, kissed the pulse that thrummed against his lips. Her unskilled fingers felt sublime as he moved his hand to slide beneath her waist, and he inwardly cursed at a knock at the door.

He ached with regret as he tied her belt and then picked up his towel, and she stood blushing and burning and wanting as he let in a frantic butler, loaded with candles and eager to ensure that their most esteemed guest was all right, explaining that the whole of London had been blacked out.

Rakhal was annoyed at the intrusion, though in the circumstance it was to be expected, and at least, he conceded, when they were alone again he'd get to start all over with Natasha and he did like her kisses. Also, the lounge room was not the most convenient of locations. He would have had to interrupt her anyway to take her to his room so that he could sheathe.

'Let us look at the view,' Rakhal suggested, for he could certainly do with some fresh air while the butler set up candles around the suite.

'What view?' Natasha asked, because all of London had been plunged into darkness. There were just a few cars on the road giving out light, a few people stepping onto the street to see what had happened. It was surreal, for it was more dark than she could ever have imagined.

'This view,' Rakhal said—and then she looked up.

The sky was a blaze of stars. The more she looked the more she saw—a swirl of masses that moved and glittered—and there were purples and blues, and the majesty of the sky she lived under was only now revealed.

'It's amazing.'

'It is nothing compared to the desert,' Rakhal said, but it was an amazing sight indeed—though his eyes had turned to her now, and he could see the white robe, could see the glitter in her eyes.

He wanted to show her the stars in the desert. He told her a little about it—that the roof of his desert abode was pulled back at night so he could sleep under the stars, as did true desert people. Not every night, he told her, but on nights when he needed to think…

And he told her a little of the land that was beautiful. He told her ear, for her body was now against him as they revisited their kiss. Except the pause had Natasha thinking—had her knowing that she needed to be brave, that there was something he needed to hear. She was embarrassed at the thought of his reaction.

'Rakhal…' She pulled back from his kiss. 'I need to tell you something…'

'You don't.'

He knew already.

'I was in a relationship…' He frowned but she could not see it. 'The thing is….' She burnt as she said it. Yes, she respected morals, but in this she had been hurt. 'I haven't slept with anyone before—he wanted to wait till we were married…'

He felt her skin burning beneath his fingers and the answer for Rakhal was simple.

'Then he should have married you.'

And Natasha had thought the same—not that she had wanted marriage to him, more that she had wanted his desire. Had wanted him not to be able to resist her. Had wanted an ardour that simply hadn't been there.

But it was here now.

'I know we come from different worlds…' She was being brave again. 'I'm not expecting…' It was terribly awkward to say to a man she had known only for one day, but Rakhal said it for her.

'I will marry someone from my land.' Rakhal was not awkward about discussing such things. 'But for now I can adore *you*.'

And he would adore her later too, he decided, for she would be his mistress. But he would not dazzle her, would not confuse her. He would tell her gently of his ways, for he was determined to keep her.

'Tonight we get to know each other, and if you are still sure in the morning…'

She was sure already.

They moved into his bedroom and he pulled back every curtain and opened all the windows. The air blew out the candles beside them until only those at the far end of the room remained. Their light lit the bed a little. He made no apology for the temperature; instead he peeled off her robe and led her to his bed.

And she shivered—but not from the cold—as he kissed her, and after a night spent tossing and turning it was a relief to lie down naked next to him.

He was so broad and so male. Her only regret was that she could not see him properly. But her hands searched him instead—the chest and the shoulders and the stomach that had teased.

His hands caressed her too as he spoke.

She wanted to know about him, wanted to know more of his mysterious ways, and even if the conversation seemed a strange one to be having as they touched each other's bodies there was a need to understand him, to learn all she could while she could, for she knew it would not be for ever.

They were facing each other, talking between kisses, his thigh over hers and his hand in her hair. His mouth was at her neck and then down at her breast, and how lucky was his future bride, to have this every night, Natasha thought as his lips nuzzled her skin. And maybe she said it, for somewhere deep in the darkness he told her he would be with his wife for just two nights a month.

'You'll only sleep together two times?'

Rakhal laughed, but it was more a low growl as he lifted his mouth from her breast. 'Much more than two times,' he explained, for he wanted her to learn his ways, wanted her back in Alzirz with him—which meant she needed a little of the truth. 'For two days and nights we will be together...'

'And then?' She could hardly breathe. His mouth was suckling at her breast, and she almost did not want him to answer for the feeling was sublime, but he lifted his lips and blew cold air onto her wet flesh before speaking.

'She will be taken away and hennaed, and then she will rest as we wait to see.'

'And then?'

His hand was on her stomach, moving towards her intimate curls. 'If there is no pregnancy she returns again when she is fertile.'

'You will hope she is pregnant, then?' Natasha said, for she would want to be back in his bed. 'So you can see each other again?'

'No,' he corrected. 'If she is pregnant then I do not see her till after the birth.'

'But…'

She could not understand, but he did try to explain. 'She will rest and be pampered.'

'I'm sure she'd rather be with you,' Natasha said, 'and you with her.' She blinked at the impossibility of it—to be married and kept apart. 'So you'd go for months…' she was more than a little embarrassed to voice it '…without…?'

'Without seeing her,' he confirmed.

'I meant…' She swallowed, for his hand was moving to her thigh now. 'Without sleeping together…' His warm fingers were between her thighs. 'Without sex…'

'Of course not.' His mouth was back at her breast, his tongue stroking it to an aching peak. 'I have my harem.'

She opened her eyes, went to push his hand away from where it was gently probing, for the thought of a harem was almost repugnant—and yet her eyes met the stars and her mind was split open. There was a tightening very low in her stomach and she wanted to hear, was strangely turned on by his ways, by the impossible ways she did not understand yet wanted to hear about.

'Tell me,' she breathed, closing her eyes to the moment.

He had felt her tense, had inwardly kicked himself for saying it too soon—for in this land his ways were not understood. But time was of the essence. One night with Natasha would not suffice, so he had to tell her more truths.

'Tell me,' she said again as his fingers parted her moist butterfly. 'Won't your wife mind…?'

'She will be relieved,' Rakhal said. 'For she will not be troubled with my needs.'

'But…'

'I will sleep only with my wife unsheathed,' Rakhal explained as his fingers slipped inside her warmth, 'and I will do this only with her…it is only she I will make come… Otherwise it would be considered unfaithful.'

There was strange honour to his ways.

'And the women in the harem…?'

'They are for me, not I for them.' He lowered his head and replaced his fingers with his mouth. 'There is none of *this*.'

And he parted her legs and gave in to himself. He would miss this. This was why he loved this land. When he went back this sweet pleasure would be only for his bride. He tasted and it felt like the last time. He probed with his tongue and felt her hands in his head and it *was* the last time, Rakhal realised, for his wife would not be so bold as to demand more from him, and nor would she weep and beg as Natasha did now.

All the tensions of the day were throbbed out into his mouth.

And afterward, she lay trying to remember how to breathe. The stars were still watching and so too were his eyes—and, no, she did not want to wait for morning.

She drank water from the carafe by the bed and could not fathom that it came from the desert. She poured some more and Rakhal drank it. She tried to rest and he tried to let her. Yet it was as though the night would not let them wait for morning; it was as though the stars had other plans for them and were willing them on.

His kiss on her shoulder made her tremble in anticipation. She could stay like this for ever, Natasha decided, as one hand played with her bottom. Still he kissed her, and then his other hand massaged her nipple. He kissed her with words while his hands were moving, stroking, assuring, telling her what she needed to hear. How, since the moment he had seen her at the police station, she had been on his mind—which, Rakhal thought, was true. How, since the moment he had met her, he had wanted her—which again, he conceded, was true.

And he said many more things—for here in this strange country, where women made simple things complicated, where they demanded declarations and promises that could never be kept, he played by the rules, gave in to the madness of the land just one more time and said things he perhaps ought not to—like how much he wanted her. Except that, too, was true.

He told her how aroused he was as she burned beneath him. He moved his tongue along her shoulders and then down to suckle at her breast, and he kissed her nipple longer, until the taste was imprinted on his tongue.

His skin was smooth and soft, his erection both compelling and terrifying—for she knew now that they would make love.

His fingers concluded that she was ready.

'Will it hurt?'

'A little,' Rakhal said as he sheathed himself.

He was over her, his erection nudging at her entrance, and he felt her tension, felt her tight and nervous. He moved his fingers down to where she was now dry.

'We don't have to…' he whispered.

'I want to,' she said, but she was honest. 'I'm scared.'

'You guide me…' he said.

And then her hand was around him, and he was so solid it terrified her more. The sheath came away in her hand.

'I will put on another…' He did not show his impatience, knew it would not help, but Rakhal was not used to anything less than seamless lovemaking. He knew that if he interrupted things now the moment would be gone. It was for that reason—that foolish, foolish reason—that he stayed.

'Just relax,' he said, for he could feel the wanting in her body at odds with the dry desert between her legs. But now, without the barrier, she had softened a little. He could feel her moist at his tip and he kissed her calmer, perhaps just a little wilder. 'Better?' he asked.

'Much.' For her panic was easing and lust was trickling back. 'I'm sorry…' She was—and embarrassed too at her cumbersomeness.

'Natasha…' She had nothing to be sorry about. He would stretch her just a little, Rakhal decided, while she was damp and more moist. 'Just a little way,' he whispered. She moaned as he stretched her, for it hurt and yet it was sublime.

He pushed and felt only physical resistance. Her mind was with his now. Gently he moved, backwards and forwards, until she begged him to enter—and he did, tearing her virgin flesh. She bit into his shoulder and he thought then he might come, was dizzy from fighting it, but of course he must not. Rakhal knew that, for he was still unsheathed.

He would come out now, he decided. Except he slid deeper inwards.

She sobbed, for, yes, it hurt. It hurt because it was almost cruel to have a man as well endowed as Rakhal as your first lover. But it was a delicious cruel, Natasha soon realised, as her body adjusted to him.

'Just a little way more,' Rakhal said, and he thought he might die from the pleasure as he felt the beckoning of her muscles dragging him in. 'Stay still,' he warned, for the soft buck of her body brought him dangerously close.

She tried to, but she had never felt anything like it, to be so completely filled, and it killed not to move with him, not to move her hips to her body's command. She gave in then, lifted her hips, and he moved out. And then as his tip neared the exit he plunged in again, for just one more taste.

He would be careful, he told himself as he sank in deeper and then did it again.

She could never have realised all she was missing out on. She felt his golden skin beneath her fingers, felt the animal passion that fought with his restraint, and the orgasm he had brought her to in the small hours was bypassed already. She could feel tension in her thighs, and low, low in her stomach, and she felt as if she might scream.

'Rakhal,' she warned, for she was so close to the edge.

'Let go,' he said, for he wanted to feel her come around his naked length.

Rakhal would not leave her in London; he wanted her in his land—she would be in his harem. He was giddy with the thought that he might have her again and again.

Natasha was giddy too. Her hips rose to his and their groins ground together; he was bucking within her, and her muscles were milking him, and Natasha found ecstasy there in his arms.

Always he loved the release, but as he came to her it was like nothing he had ever sampled before—he saw the stars in his head, the same stars that bathed the desert and shone on them tonight; he swept past Orion and pulsed deep into her.

And then he returned, back from the desert to his hotel room and to cold realisation.

He had done the unthinkable…

CHAPTER SIX

Natasha lay trying to make sense of things.

There was no excuse save insanity, which was what she felt around him. She was usually the most sensible person—reserved, some might say.

Just not with Rakhal.

His kisses, his touch, his words had taken her to places where rational thought was left behind.

After a moment he spoke.

'Natasha…what happened there…' He actually didn't know how to broach it, for this was not a conversation he had had before. This sort of thing simply did not, *could* not happen to him.

'Shouldn't have,' she finished for him. 'We didn't use anything…'

'*I* didn't,' he said. 'The mistake was mine.'

She turned and looked at him, saw the

grim set of his jaw, knew what he must surely be thinking: she had trapped him somehow. Her mind whirred for possible solutions and she breathed in relief as one flew in.

'There's a pill...' Those indigo eyes turned to her, but they were black and unreadable now. She babbled on some more, in an effort not just to reassure him but herself, as if talking could somehow erase the madness that had taken place in this bed.

He looked in silent horror at the woman he had just made love to. He accepted all responsibility for what had happened. She had been a virgin; he was a royal. He should have known better—he always knew better. Till now.

Rakhal had been raised as a leader in crisis. He must always remain calm. It had been ingrained into him, beaten into him at times, and he was grateful for those teachings now. He knew that she did not understand the implications, but Natasha's talk of a pill that could end things had adrenaline coursing through his muscles and his heart thumping in alarm.

He knew this had not been an attempt

to trap him. There was a strength to her, a dignity that suddenly unnerved him. This was a woman independent enough to go it alone. She might not even tell him about a baby—perhaps with curls of gold and its father's dark skin—and if he left now he might not even know.

Still, he did not reveal his horror. His voice was pleasant and calm when it came. 'There is time yet before you need to worry about such things.' He pulled her into his arms. 'I told you—you are to worry about nothing.'

She lay there soothed as his hand stroked her, as he told her that everything would be okay. She slept, but it was not restful, for whenever she turned or moved it was as if he were awake and his arms found her again.

At dawn she listened as the stranger who had become her lover moved to another room and chanted prayers she did not understand. And she said prayers of her own too, asking for forgiveness for her foolish mistake. It was a simple mistake. Of course they would get away with it… She heard him shower, then she heard him speaking on the phone, but it was in his own language so she didn't know what was being said.

Rakhal did not like what he heard.

Her brother was back and raging, demanding the jewels, demanding she call the police. Rakhal could not let her go back to that house. He issued instructions and did not repeat them. He only needed to say things once.

He returned, dressed in a bathrobe and unshaven. The bruise on his eye was more grey than purple now. He was still so impossibly beautiful as he sat on the edge of the bed and looked down to where she lay.

'Look…about what happened…' She wanted to discuss it properly—she wasn't actually sure that she could take a pill. She wanted to know what he was thinking. But Rakhal had other ideas.

'There is no point worrying about that now,' Rakhal said. 'Whatever happens we will sort something out. Get dressed.' He smiled down at her. 'I want to take your mind off things. I will take you to breakfast. Somewhere nice.'

'I haven't got anything suitable to wear. We could have breakfast here.'

'We could,' Rakhal said. And he pulled back the sheet and went to climb in. Then he changed his mind, smiling down at her, naked and warm.

She wriggled in delight as he traced his fingers down her hips and then paused, his eyes tenderly appraising her. 'Why don't we have breakfast somewhere a bit special?' He spoke the language of romance, the language women here seemed so badly to need, and he spoke it easily for he had had much practice. 'Paris!'

'Don't be…' Her voice trailed off, because this was his life, this was his world, and still she could not fathom it. 'I haven't got anything to wear…my passport…' It was all too impossible. 'We can't just…'

'Why not?' Rakhal said. 'I have a jet. We could be there in a couple of hours. Or lunch, maybe… I will have some clothes brought up for you…' He made the impossible so easy. 'I will send someone to get your documents, and I will have my people tidy your house. I don't want you being distressed…'

She thought of her house, the mess and the chaos she would have to return to, and she *wanted* the reprieve before she went back to her life, wanted the escape. Always around him she forgot to be sensible, and Natasha nodded her head. *Yes.*

She chose clothes from a selection from one of the hotel boutiques which Rakhal had had brought up to his suite. She chose a dress in the palest grey with a matching long coat. The hotel organised someone to do her hair and make-up too. It was the height of decadence.

The luxury of it all should have been making her giddy, but it was Rakhal who took care of that. The approval in his eyes as she came out of her bedroom and the kiss to her throat before they headed to the airport was a brief reminder of what had taken place last night. And it was not clothes or make-up she wanted. She would have happily stripped bare there and then—except Rakhal had other plans.

Plans which had swung into action. From car to plane it was seamless—for Natasha at least. There was not a hint from the staff who greeted them as to the chaos this rapid change in the Prince's plans had caused.

'Your Highness.' The robed man who had been in the car the morning she had first met him was there as they climbed on board. He bowed and kissed Rakhal's hand, and nodded his head to Natasha, then disappeared into an area towards the front of the plane.

'It's amazing!' It really was; there was a desk and large leather chairs, a bar and even a bed—it was beyond luxurious even for a hotel room, but the fact it was a plane had Natasha reeling. 'You have a *desk*?'

'I fly a lot,' Rakhal explained. 'And often I am working…' He gave her a smile. 'But not today. We should take our seats—we will be taking off soon.'

He held her hand as they taxied along the runway and took off into the morning. They would be in Paris within an hour, the captain explained once the plane had levelled out.

'I should get changed,' Rakhal said, and looked up as the steward came to take their order for breakfast. 'Just juice and pastries,' Rakhal said. 'We will be dining when we land.' He looked to his guest, supremely polite. 'If that is okay with you?'

'Of course.' She looked around the jet and he saw her eyes linger on the bed.

'Why not stretch out a little?' Rakhal suggested.

She would never have the chance to sample such luxury again, Natasha realised as Rakhal headed to the bathroom. And it was luxury to lie on the bed, to close her eyes and rest on soft pillows as the plane took her away.

It felt as if she had been sleeping for ever and the plane seemed darker when she awoke. The shutters were down. She stretched luxuriously, a little surprised when she looked over and saw Rakhal on his computer at the desk, speaking with Abdul his aide. He was not dressed in the suit she was used to. Instead he had changed into robes and had a *kafiya* on his head. Natasha's first thought was—to her shame—that she would be a little bit embarrassed walking around Paris with him dressed like that, for he looked so royal, so imposing. But even before that thought had been fully processed, even before

Rakhal turned around, the truth of her situation was slowly dawning.

'How long till we land?' Still she tried to deny the obvious—because things like this surely couldn't happen to someone like her.

'A couple of hours,' Rakhal said, and Natasha noted that he didn't even attempt to lie.

'And how long have I been asleep?'

'For a while.'

She tried to keep calm, but fear was coursing through her, and it was blind panic that had her racing from the bed to confront him where he sat.

'You can't do this.' She attempted to reason with him. 'You can't just *take* me!'

'You left me with no choice but to do so.' Rakhal was completely unmoved by her dramatics. She was starting to shout now, to beat him with her hands. He captured her wrists. 'This is about protecting what is mine.'

'I'm not yours to protect...'

'That is yet to be determined.'

And Natasha knew then it was not about *her*.

'With all that was going on, with the

things you were suggesting, I could not leave you.' To him it was logical. 'If you are pregnant with my child then I need to be certain you are taking care of yourself and that you will do nothing to jeopardise its existence. You will stay in the palace, where you'll be well looked after by women who will take the best care of you.'

'Where will you be?'

'In the desert. Soon I am to take a wife. It is right that I go there for contemplation and meditation. We will wait to see the outcome with you. You will be well taken care of, you will be looked after, and, if you are not pregnant of course you can come back home.'

She could feel hysteria rising—wanted to slap him, wanted to run for the emergency exit. But still he held her wrists. There was nothing but nothing she could do.

'And if I am?' Natasha begged, but she already knew the answer.

'If you are pregnant—' so matter-of-fact was his voice as he said it '—then there is no question that we will marry.'

CHAPTER SEVEN

IT WAS dark as they came in to land.

She could see the palace rising out of the desert, and it was the most terrifying feeling as the plane touched down in a country she hadn't even heard of till yesterday.

They had flown for hours, and when the fight in her had died Natasha had sat in a chair and stared silently out of the window. For a while she had thought they were flying over the ocean. She'd thought she could see white rippling waves. But she had come to realise that the near-full moon lit a desert beneath them. It had shown her all too clearly the remoteness of the land Rakhal would one day rule—the land he was taking her to now.

An assistant helped her into a robe that covered her from head to toe, only revealing her eyes, and once off the plane they were driven a short distance to the palace, which stood tall and exquisite, though it felt far from welcoming as she stepped out of the car. Natasha knew it would be hopeless to fight here—there was no point kicking and screaming. Even if she could get away there was nowhere to run; all she could do was stay calm and appear to have given in to him.

He was unfamiliar in his robes, dark, mysterious and forbidding, and she cursed again at her foolishness, rued the trust she had placed in him. Rakhal was flanked by several men who spoke in low voices, while Natasha was surrounded by a group of women. They walked swiftly through fragrant gardens, and only when they were safely inside the palace did Rakhal speak with her again.

'You will take refreshments with the maidens—my father has asked that I speak with him.'

For the first time she witnessed tension in his features, but his voice was as haughty and assured as ever. As he turned to go, perhaps he saw her fear, for he tried to comfort her.

'Natasha, I understand you are scared, that this must be overwhelming for you, but please know that I would never hurt you.'

'You already have,' she flared. 'Lies hurt too, Rakhal. You lied to get me on that plane—you didn't make a single attempt to speak to me, to discuss what we should do.'

'There could be no discussion—your words left me with no choice but to act.' He remained unmoved. 'Now I will speak with the King. It is not every day that a Crown Prince returns in circumstances such as this. For now you will wait.'

She had no choice but to wait, to sit as Rakhal swept out of the room, dark and unapproachable—a stranger.

Rakhal did not like to leave her.

He was more than aware how terrified she must be. Yet there had been no choice but to bring her here. Had it been any other time he could have waited things out in London, but festivities were already starting in Alzirz—their Crown Prince should be deep in the desert now, contemplating his country's future, asking the desert for guidance as he chose his future bride, not walking into his father's study to be chastised.

He was braced for a row, his back ramrod-straight, his features expressionless, as would be expected of any ruler about to go into battle. He was ready for anything as an aide opened his father's office door, braced for confrontation as he stepped inside, and yet nothing, *nothing*, could have prepared him for the sight that greeted him.

He was more than grateful for his brutal training, for the beatings he had taken in the desert, for the cruel lessons he had been forced to learn, for his mask did not slip as he laid eyes on the frail shadow of a man who had once been so strong. His voice did not waver as he greeted his father; his eyes did not shut as he watched the feeble King attempt to stand.

Rakhal kissed his father on both cheeks, as was their way, but it was not born of affection—it was simply the way that things were done.

He waited for admonishment, for his father to tell him he was a fool, but instead his father coughed, and then coughed again as Rakhal waited, his fury building towards the palace doctor, who had told him there was still much time, that they were talking months. But that was the trouble with staff who were loyal. Even an esteemed doctor did not want to face the truth at times.

The truth was in front of Rakhal.

The truth he could clearly see.

Soon he would rule.

'I thought you would go straight to the desert.' The King's voice was thin and reedy, and as he gratefully sat back down it was clear that he was growing weak.

'I will depart for there shortly.' Rakhal kept his sentence brief. There was a thickness to his throat that was unfamiliar, a sting in his nose as he looked at the man who had been so strong and proud and tried to address him as if he still was.

'So why the detour?' The King coughed again. 'You are wasting time.' He saw his son frown—the only emotion he had displayed since entering his office. 'There are only two days for coupling. You have wasted many hours travelling.'

'That is not why I brought Natasha here.' Rakhal instantly understood what his fa-

ther meant. 'I can assure you that what happened yesterday was a mistake. If Natasha
is not pregnant then I fully intend to choose
a bride from Alzirz—a woman who under-
stands our ways, who will be proud to give
birth to our future leader. The people will
not take this well—I am aware of that…'

'They will be appeased if there is an
heir.'

'Natasha would be a poor choice.' It
sounded harsh, even to Rakhal, yet it was
essential that his father understood—for
Natasha's sake as much as the country's.
Except his father had other ideas.

'You have already made your choice,'
the King interrupted. 'When you slept with
her unsheathed.'

'It was once.'

'It needs to be more.' The King held his
son's eyes. 'The desert must play its part
in this.'

For the first time Rakhal saw fear in his
father's eyes.

'We ignored its rules once—'

'Father,' Rakhal broke in. 'My mother's
death had nothing to do with that.' Logic
told him this, education told him too, and

yet in this Rakhal's voice did waver; in this Rakhal perhaps was not so strong.

'You were conceived in London,' the King said. 'None of the rituals followed. For weeks we did not know that your mother was with child. And look what happened. You, Rakhal, know better than anyone the ways of the desert cannot always be explained. I am from a lineage that is pure royal; you are from a lineage that is both royal and from the desert. Are you so brave as to test your modern theories out with your own child?'

For the first time since their meeting the King's voice was strong and he stood to confront his son.

'I was young and bold like you once. I did things my way instead of the ways of old—and look what happened. Your mother died in childbirth; you were born so small that you were not expected to survive. The desert taught us a cruel lesson, yet it gave us one chance to redeem ourselves—*you* are that chance, Rakhal. Go now and have her oiled and prepared.'

Even as Rakhal opened his mouth to protest, the King found his voice and over-ruled him.

'And tomorrow she shall be hennaed and rested.'

'It is better that she stays at the palace now.'

'No!' The King was adamant. 'Your role is that of protector—she will be terrified here without you. She shall remain in the desert with you till we have an answer.'

Rakhal was appalled at the prospect. His time before selecting a bride was for deep contemplation. At night he could give in to his body's urges, feast with the harem, and then return to the festivities and select his bride. It was unthinkable that he should have Natasha there in the desert with him—especially if he could not be with her. For it was forbidden. Once hennaed and painted, her body was not for him.

'She does not belong in the desert.'

'She does not belong in this land.'

For the first time Rakhal glimpsed his father's anger.

'However, we shall deal with the problem, not the cause. You will do well to remember that from your teachings. Perhaps your choice was not the wisest, but the people will soon forgive if it proves fruitful. If not, the people need never know…'

'Which is why you want her hidden away in the desert?'

His father was older and wiser, and still he had more answers.

'You cannot hide in the desert,' the King responded. 'My wife—your mother—told me that. The desert will always reveal the truth. There are maidens waiting for her there—they will keep me informed, as will Abdul. There will be no more discussion.'

He looked his son in the eye and Rakhal did not like what he saw there. The once black eyes were now pale and milky. But on this point his father stood strong.

'I am still King.'

'And one day I will be,' Rakhal said, but his father refused to be swayed.

'Go now,' he ordered his son. But as Rakhal reached the door he halted him. 'You have heard the news from Alzan?'

'About his twin girls?' Rakhal had far too much on his mind to smile, for now he had to tell Natasha not just that she must join him in the desert, but that tonight she must join him in his bed.

His father had had the excuse of ignorance when he had bedded his mother, had believed then that the teachings were merely fables. Rakhal did not have that excuse—his mother's death had been a warning. And yet he could not force himself on her. And it would be force, Rakhal knew. So he had far more on his mind than to engage in idle gossip.

'About his wife.'

The King's words halted Rakhal as he went to walk out. 'His wife?' Rakhal turned around.

'Rumour has it that the Sheikha Queen was most unwell during her pregnancy. That it might prove fatal were she to try and conceive again.'

'And is this from a reliable source?' Rakhal checked.

'Of course—and it had been confirmed by the most reliable,' the King said. 'Of course he did not say it directly—he never does.'

Rakhal knew who his father was refering to: the wizened old man from the desert.

'But he sees not just one test but two…
two tests that will divide us for ever or
reunite Alzanirz. Perhaps that test is the
twins. Of course Emir would not waste his
breath asking me to forgo the rules—to
allow a princess to rule Alzan.' He looked
to his son, saw despite the strong jawline,
despite the unblinking gaze, that his features were just a little pale.

'We allow a princess to rule Alzirz,'
Rakhal said. 'If Natasha is pregnant, if
the gift is a daughter, she will one day be
Queen.'

'Which is why Alzirz will go on.' The
King smiled, but then it died on his lips and
there was hate in his eyes. 'Did Emir's father revoke the rule when my wife died?'
Bitter were his words. 'No. Instead the entire burden of our country's future fell to
you, and now it is time for you to accept
that burden like a man—like the Prince
you are—and ensure our country con-
tinues. Which is why you will take this
woman to the desert and to your bed this
night.'

Rakhal walked through the palace. History lined its walls—not just portraits of

the royals, but oil paintings of the desert and the people from whom he came. He walked into the lounge where Natasha sat silent, and despite prompting by Abdul she refused to stand when he entered. All eyes except hers were on him.

'You are to come to the desert with me.'

'No.'

He heard her inhale, heard the rate of her breathing increase. 'We are leaving now.' Rakhal ignored her refusal. Abdul was watching him after all. But once they were alone he would talk to her. He would reassure her. For now he had to appear to be abiding by the rules. 'The helicopter is being prepared.'

'No!'

This time she did bite and kick and scream, but her protests were futile.

It could, as Abdul informed her, be no other way.

CHAPTER EIGHT

NATASHA had never been on a helicopter, and as it took off her stomach seemed to rise with it. She closed her eyes on a living nightmare. Abdul was on one side, and there was also a young veiled woman beside her. Rakhal sat opposite, speaking in Arabic to his aide, and she tried to shut out the words coming in over the headphones. But suddenly Rakhal spoke in English.

'To the left is Alzan.'

Natasha snapped open her eyes. 'I don't need a tourist guide.'

'I am simply trying to orientate you,' Rakhal said.

Realising that any information might help, Natasha looked out of the window. But all she could see was endless desert and panic rose within her. She could die here, right this minute, and no one would

ever know; her friends and family didn't
even know that she was here.

'There—over there,' Rakhal said some
time later, 'is my desert abode.'

As it came into view she could see a
collection of tents, but as the helicopter
hovered she saw that it was not just tents—
more a large complex. The helicopter's
spotlight, as it searched for its landing spot,
illuminated horses circling their enclosure
as the light disturbed them, and there were
camels too. But more surprising for Natasha was that there were swimming pools.
She counted three of them, right there in
the deep of the desert, and even without
the helicopter trained on them they were lit
up. Beside one there were people brightly
dressed and dancing.

Even though she had nothing to compare
it to, his desert abode was nothing like she
had expected.

Cold air hit her cheeks as Rakhal helped
her out of the helicopter. His strong arms
lifted her down and they ducked under the
blades, his grip tight on her hands. Within
two steps her shoes were lost in the sand.
She made no attempt to retrieve them.

Her footwear was simply irrelevant now. Her only thought was that she wanted to run back to the helicopter, to dive in and be lifted away. But by the time they had reached one of the tents the helicopter was already taking off into the sky.

Natasha could hear the throb of sensual music from the poolside, the sound of laughter too, and the cool air was tempered with incense. It was almost irreverent. Perhaps the servants were having a party, Natasha wondered. Perhaps they had not realised Rakhal was returning tonight.

It was quieter inside, but there was no relief to be had.

'You will put on these,' Rakhal informed her.

And though she did not want the small slippers she obliged. She wanted to be alone with him, wanted to argue away from Abdul's dark eyes that followed her every move. An argument about slippers was not high on her priorities!

'Not your robe,' Rakhal halted her as she went to take it off. 'The maidens will do that.'

Four women were approaching, their heads

lowered, bowing to Rakhal and reaching out for her. Natasha flinched. He spoke to them in Arabic and they backed away.

'Come through,' Rakhal said. 'I have told them I need to speak with you first.'

He led her through to a larger area, and thankfully the maidens did not follow. It was dimly lit and had a sensual luxury. There were cushions everywhere, and low tables heavily laden with food, and perhaps they had been expecting him after all, for there was music coming from behind a screened area and incense burnt in here too. She felt as if she was stepping into somewhere forbidden.

She was almost right. It wasn't forbidden, but it was most unusual to have a woman here with him, and Rakhal was more than a touch uncomfortable with Natasha's presence. His desert abode was not really the place he would consider bringing the potential mother of a royal heir, but circumstances had left him with little choice.

'Not you.' He turned to Abdul who, unlike the maidens, had followed them through. 'I wish to speak to Natasha alone.'

'Not tonight,' Abdul said, for on this

matter even he could pull rank with the Prince. 'I have express orders from the King.'

Rakhal hissed in frustration, for it was essential that he spoke to Natasha alone. He needed to tell her he would not harm her, would not force her into something that she did not want. But he could not say such things in front of Abdul, so he turned to Natasha, who stood pale but defiant beside him.

'Normally,' Rakhal explained, 'my wife—'

'I'm *not* your wife,' Natasha cut in.

'The potential mother of my child, then.' He was finding this difficult. Her huge green eyes were hostile and scared, and that was not how she should be at this fragile time. He *must* be alone with her, for she had no idea of the royal ways of old and she had to be seen to comply. 'Here,' he said. 'I will help you with your robe.'

'I can help myself.' She lifted it off and threw it down, stood in the dress she had chosen that morning.

The coat she had left on the plane, and the dress she had put on with such excitement was now crumpled. Her gorgeous hair was knotted from the robe and from her distress before, and her lips were swollen from crying. She looked very small, very scared, and also terribly, terribly defiant as she tossed the robe to the floor, and it evoked unusual feelings in Rakhal. He wanted to soothe her, wanted to calm her, and he crossed the room. But she shrank back, as she had with the maidens.

'Sit?' he suggested. 'Perhaps eat...'

'They'll be looking for me,' Natasha said.

'Excuse me?'

'My friends,' Natasha said. 'I do have a life. You can't just whisk me off and expect no one to notice. They'll call the police...'

'Why don't you ring them, then?' Rakhal frowned.

'Ring them?'

'I will have someone bring you a phone.' He called something in his own language and in less than a moment a maid appeared. 'There is no need for histrionics, Natasha. Ring your friends and tell them.'

'And say what?'

'The truth,' Rakhal said. She took the phone and he watched the wrestle in her eyes. 'I do not want your people worrying about you. Ring them and put their minds at rest.'

She hurled the phone at him, for he had her trapped every which way. But Rakhal had reflexes like lightning, and caught the phone.

'Ring and say you have taken a holiday,' he suggested. 'Because for now you can treat it as one. For now this is your home, and you will rest and be pampered. You will come to no harm, Natasha.' He walked over and touched her cheek. She shrank back. 'My role is to ensure you are looked after.'

He had to explain things to her—had to tell of their ways.

'If I had a bride she would live at the palace,' Rakhal explained. 'For two days I would be with her, and then the maidens would take care of her. She would be hennaed and oiled and…' Much more than that he did not know, for he would not see his wife after two days of coupling—what happened after was dealt with by women. He told Natasha the little he knew. 'She would rest and be looked after, and if the oils and the flowers did not work I would return to her the next month.'

'I don't understand.'

'You do not need to,' Rakhal said. 'The maidens know what needs to be done, how you need to be looked after, the things that must be taken care of. If you do carry the future heir there are prayers to be said, traditions that must be upheld. As I said, normally you would be at the palace. I would not see you.'

He walked to a veiled area and pulled the curtain back. After a brief hesitation she followed him. 'Here is where you will rest.' It was a lavish room of purples and reds, with a large circular bed in the centre. Above it hung a thick rope. 'You pull that and a servant will come. If you need a drink or food or a massage,' Rakhal explained. 'You may join me for conversation if I am in the lounge and the music is silent.'

'I shan't be joining you,' Natasha said, but for the first time since the plane, for the first time since realisation had hit, the tightness in her chest was abating. For the first time she felt as if she could properly

breathe. This was a room just for her, and
she stepped into it, desperate to be alone,
to gather her thoughts, to make sense of all
that had happened.

'My resting area is the other side of
the lounge,' Rakhal said, but she simply
shrugged.

She did not care where Rakhal rested.
All she wanted was to be alone—except
she froze when she heard him speak on.

'It is only tonight that you will join me
there.'

Natasha did not turn around; the tightness was back in her chest and sweat
beaded on her forehead, yet she forced her
voice calm. 'What did you say?'

'Tonight…' Rakhal kept his voice even.
Aware that Abdul was listening, he could
not reassure her. He wished she would
turn around, so she could see the plea in
his eyes, know he would not hurt her. She
might somehow understand that the harsh-
ness in his voice did not match his intent.
'You are to sleep with me tonight.'

'No…' She shuddered. 'Rakhal, no.'
Now she did turn around. She pleaded with
the man she had just met, the first man she

had made love with, who was now forcing her to join him in his bed. *'No.'*

'There can be no discussion.' He was supremely uncomfortable. Rakhal could hear the plea in her voice, but with Abdul present there was nothing he could do. 'Go now,' Rakhal said as the maidens approached. 'They will have you prepared.'

CHAPTER NINE

RAKHAL lay on the bed, waiting for the maidens to bring Natasha to him.

Music was softly playing and he could hear the sound of water and the maidens' chatter as they bathed her. She did not return their conversation. He could see the occasional glimpse of her shadow on the white tented ceiling, could see locks of her hair and the curves of her body, and he did his best not to look at the teasing images. For though the room had been prepared, though the music and the scents had been chosen carefully to arouse, he knew he must resist.

They hadn't been alone since their time back at the hotel. There had been no chance to explain things. Natasha would never have agreed to come with him, and neither could he have left her in London to deal with her brother alone—especially if there was a chance she was carrying his child.

He had never thought she would be brought to the desert. It had not entered his head that his father would insist on this night. But at least in his bed, alone, he could finally speak with her, reassure her.

But Natasha dreaded his bed. She could see his shadow on the ceiling as the maidens bathed her, and though last night had been wonderful she could not stand the thought of sleeping with him now—could not give in without a fight.

Natasha climbed out of the bath and shivered as the maidens oiled and dressed her in the flimsiest of gowns, and then led her through the tent towards his resting area. She willed fear to subside so that she might think.

'I need my jewels,' Natasha said, for they had been taken from her. She turned to the maidens. 'If I am to be presented to him I need to wear my jewels.'

'They are in your chambers,' Amira, a maiden who spoke a little English, informed her. 'They are safe there.'

'You don't understand. They were my

mother's,' Natasha said. 'And my grand-mother's. It is tradition that I should be wearing them.'

Amira gave a nod and led her to her room. Tradition was the one word that seemed to reach her.

'And I need to pray,' Natasha said, 'before I put them on.'

Amira nodded and stepped outside as Natasha got down on her knees. She knew she had but a few minutes, and for the first time she was glad she had been brought to the desert—for here the walls were not made of stone, and she knew that this was her only chance.

Rakhal waited and he waited, trying to plan what he would say to her, how best he could make her understand. He knew she was out of the bath, had thought she should be with him now, but then this was unusual for him too. So he listened to the soft music, lay back on the bed. It was then that he heard the commotion, watched as a curtain parted.

But instead of Natasha, a panicked maid called out to him, 'Your Highness!' There was fear in her voice and already he was standing, whipping a sash from the bed as the maiden spoke on. 'She is not here.'

Rakhal demanded more information.

'She asked to go to her room, to collect her jewels. She insisted that she wear them for you.'

And Rakhal knew then that she had run, that the jewels had been an excuse, but that she would not have left them behind.

'She said she wanted to pray...I should not have left her alone...' The maiden sobbed for his forgiveness. 'I never thought she would run,' Amira begged, for only a mad person would run into the desert at night. Or a person who did not know how impossible it was to survive.

For the first time, Rakhal did not wait to be dressed. He pulled on his robe and sandals as the maids summoned help from the guards. When they heard Natasha had gone missing the staff, unused to such strange behaviour, ran for their horses and Jeeps, but Rakhal halted them. Somehow he kept his head, ordered them to collect lanterns and to search on foot. He did not want them racing off into the night; he did not trust that they would brake in time, and nor did he trust the horses not to trample her. That sort of search could only take place at dawn.

By then it might be too late.

No one ran into the desert night—especially dressed in a flimsy gown. Did she not understand how cold it was out there? That the winds that brought heat to the sands by day chilled them at night? That the scorpions would be out now, ready to bite at her bare feet? That even if the sand shone white beneath the moonlight and stars she would be lost before she knew it? The seemingly flat sands were dunes that shifted and changed like the ocean. The wind would carry her screams not to him but through the canyons, for the desert was especially cruel to strangers.

He did not wait for the others to gather; instead Rakhal strode into the night, shouting out her name. But then it dawned on him that Natasha was running from him. That she would rather flee into the harsh, unforgiving desert then spend a night with him. And he ceased shouting, silently asking the skies for a chance to explain, a chance to tell her that he never would have forced her, that that had not been his intent.

After fifteen minutes of running—to where she did not know—the adrenaline left Natasha, and she fell exhausted onto the cold sand. She knew that she had been crazy to run, but it had proved equally impossible to stay, simply to submit. She could hear shouts far in the distance and realised the pack was heading in a different direction, that she still had a chance to escape. Natasha looked out, to the vast space that would surely claim her, then looked back to the tent. But already it had disappeared from her vision and the voices were fading into the distance. It was either call out now and summon help, only to be returned to him, or take her chance with the night...

She chose hope.

Rakhal watched from a distance. He saw her turn, resisted the urge to call out to her, and watched as she made up her mind, as she turned from the voices that would bring her to him and faced the dark instead. It was then that he called out, his voice making her still for a second and then propelling her into a run.

'You would rather step into the night than be returned to me?'

'Yes!' Still she tried to run, but he soon caught up. He grabbed at her wrist and his grip was too strong. He spun her round.

'Even when I tell you I would never hurt you? That I will take care of you?'

'I don't need to be taken care of!' Natasha screamed, kicking and hitting and trying to bite—because, yes, she *would* rather take her chances alone in the desert than be taken care of in that way.

'But you do!' Still he gripped her wrist. He knew the hissing and sparks would fade like a firecracker and he did not argue further, just held on to her as she spun in anger, as she cursed and shouted. Finally it faded, and he let her go when spent; she sank to the sand and sat hugging her knees, and then she looked up at him and with all she had left in her she spat.

She missed.

Even defeated, Rakhal noted, she did not cry, and there was a twist in his chest, a rare need to reach out and touch. But as he tried he saw her head pull away, and then angry eyes flashed towards him.

'Do it, then!' She went to pull off her gown. 'I won't give you the satisfaction of my fighting.'

He was appalled at her thoughts, that she believed he would treat her as such. He sank to the ground and pulled at the gown, the flimsy material tearing as he fought to keep it on. 'Stop this!'

'Why? We both know what's going to happen. Just take me here and I can vomit in the sand rather than in your bed.'

'I am not going to sleep with you.' Still she fought. 'I would never force you…'

'Oh, please,' Natasha hurled. 'I was being prepared for you.'

'Because the maidens cannot know that we do not sleep together, that I have no intention…' She paused for just a moment, ceased fighting just long enough for him to go on. 'Abdul cannot know that I have only the best intentions,' he explained, 'which is why I could not speak properly with you on the plane. You were in danger back in London. I had no choice but to bring you here.'

'Danger!' She shot out a mirthless laugh. 'You think that was danger?'

'Your brother came back in the night,' Rakhal said. 'He broke windows. He was raging… Do you think I would leave you to deal with that?'

'I'd have dealt with it!'

'How?'

She didn't know—she actually didn't know. Her heart seemed to squeeze tight with fear, for had she not met Rakhal, had she not been with him that night, she would have been dealing with her brother's rages. Her hand went to her mother's necklace. She knew her brother would have ripped it from her throat, and even if she was angry with him, she was scared for him too.

'Was he arrested?'

'No.' He was sitting with her now. Her gown was torn and her breast was exposed, but he pulled up the fabric and held it as he spoke. 'He ran off, but he came back in the morning, remorseful. By then we were already on the plane. I had left instructions. My people have dealt with him.' She started to panic again, to grapple to escape him, but he held her still, kept her covered, and realised just how little she trusted him, how little she knew of their ways. 'Your family is my concern too!' Rakhal shouted above her rage. 'Your brother is on his way here.'

'Here?'

'He was made an offer,' Rakhal explained. 'His debts paid, including yours, in return for six months labour in the mines of Alzirz.'

'The *mines*!' What was this place? What were they doing to Mark? But she did not know him.

'He will leave here a wealthy man. He will work hard for six months and build muscle instead of debt. He will eat food from my land and be nourished. He is not here as a slave—he is here to rebuild his life. You can speak with him soon. And—' Rakhal revealed his deeper motivation '—if you are not pregnant, when you return to London you will have six months to sort out your life…'

His voice trailed off and Natasha sat silent, trying to take in all he had told her. And despite her fears, despite her confusion, there was a bud of calm inside her;

the fear that had fluttered for months, maybe longer, was quietly stilled. Finally her brother had a chance.

'I would never hurt you. All this I was going to tell you when you were brought to me tonight.'

For the first time since the plane she could properly look at him. For the first time since then he was the man she had met—except she understood a little more of his power now, and could see, too, the foolishness of her ways. For, yes, she had been a virgin, but she shared the responsibility and so too the consequences.

'Rakhal, I accept my part in our night together.' She swallowed. 'I accept that if I am pregnant then there will be a lot of decisions that need to be made. But I simply can't try to *get* pregnant.' Her voice was urgent. 'Which is what tonight would have been about—'

'I understand that,' Rakhal interrupted. He believed in tradition, and he believed in the desert, but he was modern in other things, and in this he would defy his father, in this he would turn his back on the desert rules. 'We would not have….' Now it was he who hesitated. 'We would not have made love. I too am prepared to accept the fate we made that night.'

He looked at her and slowly she nodded, starting to believe that the man she had met was still there inside him.

'When I brought you here it was my intention that you stay at the palace. Only when I arrived my father instructed that we go to the desert, that all the rituals must take place. Here it is unthinkable that you would not want to be carrying the heir to the throne. The people could never understand that we are both hoping you're *not* pregnant. We need to let them think that we are trying to ensure that you are.'

'So we are just to share a bed?' Natasha verified. 'Nothing else will happen?'

'It is not as simple as that. They need to think…'

He was embarrassed, Natasha realised.

'They need to hear,' he explained. 'The maidens will wait outside the sleeping area.'

'We're to make *noises*?' She couldn't believe what she was hearing. 'You are going to pretend to be making love to me?'

He nodded.

'But the shadows....' She thought of his shadow, taunting her on the tent ceiling as she bathed. 'They'd see them.'

'They will see our shadows and we will look as if we are. But I give you my word, Natasha, it will be for appearances only.'

She believed him.

She looked into eyes that were the same colour as the sky above and knew he was giving her his word.

'Some people condemn our ways. That is from ignorance. If you are carrying my child, you are the most precious person in this land.'

There were shouts in the distance. Natasha could see lights in the shadows and people nearing, and no more did she want to run and take her chances with the night.

'When this is over, if you are not carrying my child, still I will look after you. You will have a stamp in your passport that will speak volumes—a stamp that only I as Crown Prince can give. I will make sure your brother gets on well, and you will be able to visit him freely. I know I have done little to earn it, but I am asking for your trust.'

He could not have all of it, but finally there was hope for her brother when before there had been none. And she accepted, too, even if she could not fully understand, how impossible it would have been for him to leave her in London if she was carrying his child.

'I'm angry,' she warned him. For even if she trusted him a little there was a deep fury still there. 'I'm *so* angry.'

'I know that,' Rakhal said. 'But for to-night can you find a way to put that on hold? If we can placate the people—if we can appear to go along with things—then more and more we will be left alone.'

Tears glistened in her eyes as she nodded her head. Rakhal called to his people that he had found her and picked her up and carried her to his tent. The tears that threatened were not born of fear, but of the knowledge that the strong arms holding her, his need to protect her, the care he was taking, had nothing to do with her. He cared only so long as there might be a child.

CHAPTER TEN

THE maidens gave her a drink and some fruit and then bathed her again, paying careful attention to the scratches on her legs and gently chiding her in their own language. They dabbed at her wounds before dressing her in a fresh gown and then she was led through the tent. There was music playing and the lighting was low. She could see the shadow of Rakhal through the tent wall and swore if she ever was his wife that this would be the first thing to change.

The maidens left her at the threshold of his sleeping quarters and then took their places on the floor. She was relieved rather than scared to see him this time—relieved to leave the maidens and their strange rituals behind.

Or she was relieved until she saw the

man that awaited her, for he seemed even more beautiful than the last time. It was as if her brain were incapable of recording such exquisiteness in detail. He was lying on a vast bed, or rather a raised area that was draped in furs and silks. The space was all male—from the dark colour scheme to the woody fragrance that burnt. It was clearly not an area for sharing; clearly this was *his* domain. Rakhal was on his side, naked except for a sliver of silk covering his groin. His chest and his limbs had been oiled too, and his skin gleamed in the candlelight. And now Natasha was more nervous than the virgin she had been when first she had shared his bed.

Then his promise had been to please her.

Now it was not to.

He took her hand and guided her onto the bed, moving his head in close to hers and murmuring into her ear. 'It will be okay.'

'I know.'

She could smell the pomade in his hair, as she had during their first kiss, but things were so very different this time.

'We should kiss,' Rakhal said, and he

captured her face in his hands and brought her close.

But their mouths did not move, just their heads, and she trusted him a little more still. Then his hands went down her arms, and now their lips did meet—but it was just lips, and they did not press. He moved his head to her ear and she felt his breath. They stayed for a moment, his hands running along her arms, caressing her, then moving to her back as if pulling her in, and then to her front, where they rested still between them. She trusted him a little more.

'I should take off your gown now.'

She nodded her consent, lifted her arms, and he slid it over her head. They knelt facing each other. As she shook her hair she caught sight of her own shadow, could see her hard nipples, his fingers appearing to trace them—yet they did not touch her. Even when he lowered his head and seemingly kissed her breast his mouth stayed closed, and his tongue did not cool the heat. She ached for it to do so and performed for the shadows—or was it for herself?

Her neck arched back and the music quickened—their shadows, Natasha realised, were for the musician, for the tempo changed as she and Rakhal moved. The strings of the *quanoon* seemed to pluck deep inside her as his chin grazed her breast and his kiss on her skin remained elusive. Her hands moved to his head—to steady herself, she told him.

And he steadied her too—one hand around her waist and the curve of her bottom—and the music hastened and she rested a head on his shoulder. She could feel her breasts flatten on his chest and tried to slow down her breathing.

'Now,' Rakhal said, 'you must trust me.'

He laid her down and she stared at the wall, at the outline of his body and the full state of his arousal. Of course he was aroused, Natasha told herself. She was too—not that she would let him know it. It was just two bodies confined—two bodies primed with food and scents and brews for this moment—two bodies that last night had been so deliciously intimate. It would be impossible for him not to be aroused.

He lifted her knees and lowered his head between her legs—but his mouth did not touch her. She could feel only his breath when she wanted his tongue. It was a relief when he told her to make some sounds of approval, to let it be known that the Crown Prince Sheikh was arousing her.

She moaned not because she was told to, but because she had to. And as his hair met her thigh, as his head danced between her legs, it was torture that his mouth did not caress her. He pulled her hand to his head, told her to moan louder, told her to raise her hips. As she did so she misjudged, felt for a second the soothing of his mouth, and then he moved back, and she bit down on a plea for him to continue as the music urged him. She was acting, she told herself as his head rose.

She was acting, Natasha insisted as he lay over her.

'Soon,' Rakhal said, 'you can rest.'

His voice was hoarse. His weight was on his elbows, but their groins still met and his erection was pressed between them. She didn't want to be resting—she wanted him inside her.

'Say my name,' he said. 'You would call my name.'

And she did. She called his name as if he *were* inside her.

'And again,' Rakhal said as he moved over her.

She sobbed it out, saw their shadows moving in unison, and the music hastened and urged them on to a place she must not go.

'Trust me,' he said.

And she wished she didn't—wished he were a liar and would take her now.

The music and the potions must have confused her senses, must have muddled her brain, for as she lay trapped beneath him, as she watched their images move on the tent wall, she wanted to stay there, wanted to be having his baby, wanted for ever with Rakhal. But it would not always be like this, she reminded herself. The wife of Rakhal would be kept far removed from him—if she were having his child, after the wedding she would not see him. So she tore her eyes from the wall and looked up to the sky. Only that did not dilute her arousal. Tonight, quite literally, she saw stars.

'Rakhal!' She said his name for she wanted this over. She could not play this dangerous game. 'Rakhal,' she begged, and he moved faster as the music reached a crescendo.

'Now,' he said in her ear and he lifted his body and shuddered a moan and faked his first orgasm. Without his bidding she called out, as she had last night. Should he kiss her? Rakhal wondered. If she were his bride, would he kiss her now?

Perhaps he forgot for a moment that they were acting, and for Natasha it was a relief that he did.

His tongue was a cool balm, and while their rocking was slowing, the music fading, it was contrary to the fire in their groins. It should be over—and yet his erection was still pressing, his breathing was ragged, and her fingers were on his back and digging in. Her hips rose higher against him and his tongue darted in a decadent tryst. Natasha tried to quiet the jerks of her body, tried to tell herself she was playing only the necessary game. But as he lifted his head and watched the colour rise from her chest to her cheeks, as he felt tense beneath him, there was a glimmer of triumph in his eyes as she denied her orgasm.

He rolled off her and onto his side, pulled the silk over his groin, and Natasha closed her eyes, guilty at having enjoyed it.

'Well done,' Rakhal whispered. 'Now you can rest, and tomorrow you will be taken to your own room. We don't have to be together after this night…'

His voice trailed off as a maiden entered, and she was reminded of her role as Rakhal translated the maiden's words.

'She is asking that you lift your hips.'

And she burnt with shame as she did so and a cushion was placed under her, to tilt her hips so that the supposed royal seed might get its best chance.

A vessel—that was all she was, Natasha reminded herself.

All she would ever be to him.

And she closed her eyes to the stars and tried to hold onto her tears as she waited for morning to come.

CHAPTER ELEVEN

Her time with the master was over, Amira informed her.

Natasha had not slept; instead she had lain pretending to. When Rakhal had risen at sunlight to pray she had opened her eyes to see the maidens quietly waiting. She'd been led through the tent to eat flat bread and dates. She'd drunk infused tea and now they bathed her.

She would never relax, Natasha was sure. But the water smelt of lavender, and the fingers that massaged her scalp were firm and yet tender, and as she breathed in the fragrant steam Natasha felt the tension seep from her. She understood that she was being taken care of, that the maidens meant her no harm.

She was taken to lie on low cushions and her breath was in her throat as Amira explained that she would be decorated. Her skin was damp and warm as tiny leaves and flowers were painted around her areola and just above her pubic bone. The tiny flowers dipped above and into her intimate curls, and Amira did her best to put Natasha at ease as she explained their ways. An old lady drew a circle and then darkened one sliver. When she pointed to the sky Natasha understood it was last night's moon that had been drawn—the time recorded.

'For nine of these moons we shall paint you and pray that the flowers will grow to here.' Amira pressed into the middle of Natasha's ribcage and the old lady said something. Amira laughed. 'Sometimes ten moons,' Amira translated, and then the old lady said something else—only this time the maidens bowed their heads.

'What is she saying?'

'She speaks of Queen Layla,' Amira explained. 'The flowers only climbed to here.' She pointed to just above Natasha's umbilicus. 'There were only six moons for our Prince. It was too soon,' Amira explained, then tried to reassure her. 'But it will not happen to you. Queen Layla was not safe in Alzirz at her fertile time. She was not painted and fed the potions. She did not have us to take care of her...'

'Where was she?'

Amira looked uncomfortable and did not answer immediately; instead she carried on with her artwork. After a moment she spoke on. 'She was from the desert, and when she was in the palace she pined for it. She was so thin and so ill, and she was growing weaker... She joined the King in London—he wanted to try the doctors there.' Amira pulled a face. 'She would have been safer here. Instead she came back to us already carrying a babe. They nursed her at the palace; they did everything that could be done. But she was too weak...'

Natasha was starting to understand their terror of breaking any traditions. When the decorating had been completed, she was oiled again till she was drowsy, then dressed in sheer organza and led to her bed. She was given a thick milk and honey drink, but it was sickly and sweet and she could not finish it.

'You must drink it all,' Amira said. 'It will help you to sleep.' She gave a smile. 'You will sleep now till tomorrow morning.'

When she was left alone Natasha put down the goblet, unsure what they were giving her, and unsure if it was okay if she were pregnant. She knew there was no way she would sleep for twenty-four hours, but the room was dark and cool and finally she did fall asleep—only to awake disorientated. The room was still dark, and she could hear music filtering through from the lounge. Without thinking she wandered out.

'What are you doing here?' Immediately Rakhal stood from the cushion he was lying on. 'You do not come out when the music plays!'

He was harsher than he'd intended, but she must not come out when there was music, for it masked other sounds. To his credit, he had just been sitting pondering—but Natasha was not to know that. More than that, the sight of her unsettled him—this side of a woman he was not sup-

posed to see. Her hair was oiled and her
skin was too; the organza robe was flimsy
and clung to her. She was lush and ripe and
he was wanting. But she had been bathed
and painted.

'Go to your room!' he snapped, and
promptly led her back. 'You do *not* come
out when the music is on.'

'Then turn it off,' Natasha said, and
looked at him, this man who would send
her back to her room. 'Actually, don't
bother.' She shook her head. 'I don't even
want to talk to you anyway.'

'Sleep,' Rakhal ordered.

'I can't sleep.'

'Pull the rope.'

He turned away, for he must rise above
his feelings. She was completely forbidden
now, and he was stronger than his urges, so
he led her to her room. He saw the goblet
still full on the tray on the floor.

'You need to drink that.' He crossed the
room and picked it up.

She sat on the edge of the bed and he
held it to her lips. She loathed it. It was
sickly and thick like custard, and it ran
down her chin, but his fingers caught it.

'All of it,' Rakhal said. 'There are herbs that help you to rest, that are good for your womb.'

He pressed the thick goo to her lips and she took it from his finger. He was hard and trying to ignore it.

He pulled back the silk and she slid into bed. Her body was on fire. It must be the herbs or the oils, for there was heat between her legs and her breasts felt taut as he stared down at her.

'Sleep,' he ordered, and left the room.

So tempted was she to call him. And it was the strangest place, the most dizzying place, for the music was louder from the lounge and it lulled her. The herbs from the drink made her dreams giddy, and then the music was quiet, and there was just the sound of laughter drifting across the desert night. A splash from the pool and then another one. She opened her eyes and a tear escaped—for it was not, as she had thought when she'd first arrived, the servants partying while the master was away.

She had only just realized. The bright colours the women had been dressed in, the dancing, the laughter that had come from the pool...

That was his harem.

CHAPTER TWELVE

'You can continue to sulk,' Rakhal said a few days later, when she was still so furious she would hardly speak with him, 'or you can enjoy the reprieve.'

'I'll sulk, thank you.'

Natasha lay on the cushions. She was allowed out, apparently, because the music wasn't playing. She was still dressed in the flimsy organza, and would be bathed at sunset tonight. Rakhal had dismissed the maidens who usually hovered around her, and satisfied that the coupling had taken place Abdul left them alone now, but although they now had the opportunity, Natasha refused to talk.

'You wanted a holiday...'

'I wanted to lie on the beach and spend time with my friends.'

'But you weren't able to,' Rakhal reminded her, 'for your brother stole from you. Now you can rest and be pampered. I do not see what your issue is.'

'Issues,' Natasha corrected. She was angry at him on so many levels—so many and especially one—but she could not bring herself to speak about it, could not swallow down her jealousy enough for it not to appear in her voice. So she spoke of other things that bothered her—and there were plenty! 'You brought me here against my will.'

'You gave me no choice,' Rakhal said. 'When you spoke of this pill that you could take.'

Natasha looked away. Really she was not sure that she would have taken the pill—wasn't sure of anything any more—but Rakhal did not leave things there.

'Did you think I would leave you to deal with your brother?'

He had a point, but she would not give in. 'You could have discussed things with me.'

'There was no time.' Rakhal had no choice but to admit it. 'I explained to you that one day I would marry. I had already been told to return to choose my bride. I was to fly out on the Monday.'

And he watched the anger grow in her, watched the fire on her cheeks, and there was rare guilt as she challenged him.

'So I was your last fling?'

'I hoped,' Rakhal said, 'to see you again…'

'Were you going to ask me to join your harem?' she spat.

'I knew that would not go well. I thought I might see you in London.' She tried to rise from the cushions but he stood over her. 'Do you understand that I could not leave you in London knowing that you might be carrying my child? That I could not marry another without first being sure you were not? If you are pregnant,' Rakhal said, 'it might be my country's only chance to continue. My father was once arrogant, assuming he would produce many heirs.'

She sat there swallowing her fury as he continued.

'If you are pregnant,' Rakhal explained, 'I know it will be a difficult transition for you—that much I do understand. However, you will never live in fear again, and you will never know anxiety—that is my duty to you…I take care of your family. I take care of your problems. You live in luxury; you raise your children.'

'Without you?'

'You would see me through your fertile times,' Rakhal explained, 'and for feasts and celebrations, and of course I would come regularly and visit the children, teach them our history—especially the eldest.'

He did not understand the tears in her eyes—had never had to try to explain this before. He snapped his fingers. He was uncomfortable with this conversation and he did not like to discuss the pointless—for these were things that could never change.

'I am going to bathe and then I will walk in the desert,' Rakhal said. 'You should rest.' And he ordered music which meant she must return to her room.

She lay there for almost an hour seething, hearing the sound of laughter that came from the bathing area. No, she would not meekly lie back and accept his ways—at least in certain things!

'What are you doing here?' Rakhal snapped as she walked into his bathing area and the laughing and chatter abruptly ceased. 'I am bathing.'

'Really?' Her eyes flashed their warning and her voice chilled the room. 'Tell your maidens they are dismissed.'

Rakhal's eyes were just as angry, but with a few short words and a flick of his wrist they were left alone. As he had stood over her before, Natasha now stood over him.

'I'm here because you think I may be pregnant. You are considering taking me as your bride.' She spoke very slowly, her face coming close to his. 'And you have the gall to have three women wash you while I am sent to my room…'

'I was having a bath.' Rakhal was far from repentant. 'There is nothing sensual in it.'

She slipped her hand in the water and found his thick, warm tumescence. 'Oh, I beg to differ.'

He moved her hand away. She was decorated, he remembered. But he saw her pale fingers linger on the surface of the water and wanted to push her hand back down.

'You are to rest…'

'I'm bored with resting.' Her eyes were dangerous. 'And I tell you this now, Rakhal—you have your rules, well, here are mine. There are to be no other women—and that means no maidens bathing you.' She saw his jaw tighten and she glimpsed a possible future and did not like it. 'If I am pregnant that will go for our marriage too.'

'You are being ridiculous.'

'No.' She shook her head.

'You will be in the palace,' he told her. 'You will not even know…'

'I'll know,' Natasha said.

Rakhal did not like the rules being re-written—especially this one—and simply dismissed her.

'Fine,' Natasha said. 'I'm going for a walk.'

'A walk!' He was aghast. 'You do not walk. You are to rest.'

'I have rested.' She was having great trouble keeping her voice reasonable. 'And now I would like some fresh air. I want to see the desert.'

'It is not a place for a stroll,' Rakhal said, but she would not give in.

'If you want to swim I have a private pool, and there is a garden around it…'

'I want to get out.'

'You do not just wander out to the desert alone. I thought the other night had taught you that much at least…'

'Then walk with me.'

If she stayed inside, even within the compound, for another minute she would surely go crazy. Perhaps he sensed that, for he gave a nod, and as he began to call the maidens to come and dry him and dress him he had the good sense to change his mind.

'Go and put on a robe,' Rakhal said. 'And you must have a drink before we leave.' Still she stood there. 'I'm assuming you're not here to dry me?'

Her blush chased her out of the bathroom. It was not what he had said, more the thoughts his words had triggered. She refused to think of him drying and dressing, took the small victory that he was alone, and slipped on a robe over her sheer gown. The maids came and tied on thin leather sandals, ensured she took a long drink, clearly worried that she was leaving the safety of the tent.

'I'll be fine,' she assured Amira, but she could see the dart of fear in the young girl's eyes.

As soon as she was outside she understood why, for the air was not soothing. It was hot and dry. Even the light wind cast sand in her eyes, and she realised then the haven of the compound.

'It is not a place for walking,' Rakhal said.

'I thought you said you went out in the desert a lot? That the desert is where you do your thinking…?'

'I am from the desert, though.'

'You mean your mother was from the desert.'

He looked down to where she walked beside him. 'It is not that simple—even if I never met her, her history is within me. I know how to survive here. You do not.'

'What was she like?' Natasha asked. 'You must have found out…'

Rakhal had never discussed this sort of thing—not even with his father. His childish questions had been dismissed. Yet he had found out things on his visits to the desert, and had overheard conversations with the maidens—yes, his mother had been a wise and beautiful soul, but she had been other things too, and he chose now to share them.

'She was very unusual,' Rakhal said. 'My father met her when he was walking; he found her dancing in the desert. He chose her as his bride even though he was warned against it. Normally the King's wife does not cause problems, but my mother did.'

'Tell me,' Natasha urged—not just because she had to understand this complicated man, but because the desert fascinated her so.

'My father had work to do in London. After a few months of marriage he was disappointed that my mother was not pregnant and she was too—she did not like the palace and pined for the desert. The maidens were frantic, for she stopped eating and would hardly take a drink—she spat out the custard...' He turned and gave a wry smile, for Natasha had done the same. 'She grew too thin, too pale and weak, and my father had her taken to London. He said that there the best hospitals were available, the best treatments, and once there she started to pick up and eat…'

'Maybe it was your father she missed and not the desert?'

Rakhal shook his head, but he could not completely refute it. After all, it was in London that he had been conceived.

'My father carries guilt with him—he should not have succumbed with his bride in London. None of the traditions were followed. She returned to Alzirz already pregnant. She stayed at the palace but despite their best efforts the damage was done and she grew weaker there. I was born just a few months later and she died in the process.' He looked over to Natasha. 'I do not ask you to believe in our ways, just that you understand that in going through with this I am trying to protect you too.'

And that much she did understand.

'I spoke to my brother today.'

She had at first thought herself a prisoner, and had been surprised on the second day when Amira had brought her a phone and said that her brother wished to speak with her—now they spoke most days.

'How was he?'

'He said sorry,' Natasha said. 'He's said sorry many, many times. But this time I think he means it.' She glanced up at Rakhal, to his strong profile, to the eyes she could not read. She wanted to ask him a question. 'I've been thinking…'

'The desert makes you think.'

'I know,' she admitted. 'I was so angry with my parents for making me sell the house…' her words tumbled out fast '…I think they were looking out for me—I think they knew Mark's problems. If the house had been in both our names….' She shuddered at the thought.

'They still are looking out for you,' Rakhal said.

'Do you believe that?'

'Of course.'

'Do you think your mother is looking out for you?'

Those wide shoulders shrugged and she almost had to run to keep up with him, but then he paused. 'Have you heard of dust devils?'

She shook her head.

'Tornado?'

She nodded.

'Sometimes there are small ones. Often...'
He looked out to the horizon, as if looking might make one appear. 'Sometimes I think I see her there dancing,' Rakhal said. 'Sometimes I hear her laughing. It was five years ago that my father insisted I marry.' He looked at her shocked face and smiled. 'Here in Alzirz we only marry once in a lifetime.'

'So you've defied him?'

'It was not easy,' Rakhal said. 'There was much pressure. I know my people need an heir. I came out here to think and I heard her laughing, as if she was giving me her blessing to refuse. Maybe I am wrong. Maybe I should have married then...' He looked to Natasha. 'It might have saved you some trouble.'

He was uncomfortable with this discussion—had told her things he had never shared. He started to walk on.

'Anyway, she is back with the desert she loved.'

'Rakhal.' She looked out at a landscape that was fierce, brutal and staggeringly beautiful, and then she looked back to a man that was the same. She craved his mouth and his mind, but not his ways. 'It wasn't the desert she pined for—it was your father.'

'Enough!'

'Well, clearly they were happy to see each other in London.' She would not be silenced. 'I can think of nothing worse than being locked away in the palace. Especially...' Natasha swallowed. 'Especially if I loved my husband and knowing...' She could not bite down on her venom, for how she hated his ways. 'Your mother would have loathed knowing he was with his harem.'

'I said that is *enough*.' Rakhal did not need a lecture from a woman who had spent just a few nights in his land. 'You admonish our ways, yet you defend yours. In my country women are cosseted, looked after—whereas you were in fear of your own brother. And,' he demanded, 'is there fidelity in your land?'

'Some,' Natasha said.

'Rubbish,' Rakhal said. 'In your land hearts get broken over and over because of the impossible rules. Here we accept that no one woman can suffice for a king. I will not continue with this ridiculous conversation,' Rakhal said, and strode off.

'You really don't like arguing, do you?' She ran to keep up with him. 'You only like it when I agree with you. Well, I never will.'

'You might have to.'

'No.'

She stopped and stood still in the fierce heat. She stood as he walked, and she called to his back as he walked on.

'If I am to respect your ways, then you will respect mine.'

'Natasha, we do not have time for this. The sun is fierce. It is time to return to the tent.'

'I'm not going back until you listen to me.'

'Then you will be waiting a very long time.'

But of course they both knew he was bluffing, for though he would allow Natasha to perish in the desert, she might be carrying his child and that made it a different matter indeed.

With a hiss of annoyance Rakhal turned

around and strode towards her. 'I will carry you back if I have to.'

'Good,' Natasha said. 'Then my mouth will be closer to your ear.'

Reluctant was the laugh that shot from his lips. 'You have an answer for everything.'

'No, Rakhal, I don't,' Natasha admitted. 'I have no idea what is going to happen if I *am* pregnant. I don't have any answers there. But while we wait and see what is going to happen, while I'm stuck here in the middle of nowhere, while I am forced to play by your rules, then I insist on enforcing one of mine. There will be no other women.'

'Natasha.' His voice was full of reason—patient, even—as he explained the strange rules. 'I have told you: I cannot sleep with you if there is even a chance you are pregnant...'

'Then you'd better get used to being alone.' She saw the shake of his head. 'I mean it, Rakhal.'

'Suppose I play by your rules? What if you *are* pregnant? What if we are to be wed? You'd really expect me to go months, maybe a year...'

'You clearly expect *me* to.'

'But it is different for women,' Rakhal said. 'You went almost a quarter of a century without it. After all, you—'

He did not get to finish. Her hand sliced his cheek and he felt the sting of her fingers meet his flesh.

'If I am your wife, you are loyal to *me*.'

'And if I am not?' Rakhal challenged. 'What? You will lie there rigid like a plank of wood?' The triumph she had witnessed that night was back in his eyes now. 'I did not even touch you the other night, yet your body came to me...'

'You hadn't been with another,' Natasha retorted. 'You didn't sicken me...*then*.' And the wind whistled across the desert, the sun seemed to burn in the back of her skull, as she told the truth. 'I would never forgive you, Rakhal.' She made things a little more clear. 'And I don't give out second warnings.'

CHAPTER THIRTEEN

SHE could not sleep, despite the custard.

Eight days here and she was growing more crazy by the day.

Her breasts felt tender and she wondered if she would soon have her period, but—more worryingly for Natasha—she wasn't so sure that she wanted it to arrive. She wanted more time with Rakhal.

She should not enjoy their conversations, she told herself.

Should not crave the evenings when they played old board games or ate and laughed or simply talked. Should not lie at night and listen to the music and remember the shadows and picture herself back in his bed.

Should not let herself fall in love with this strange land...

And when the music was silenced she wished she could sleep, wished that she did not crave his company, so she lay there, though she had been given permission. She should not condone his strange summons—except she could not sleep.

'What are these?' She had never seen anything more beautiful. There was a roll of black velvet on the floor and it was littered with jewels of all different shades of pink, from the palest blush to the darkest of wine, and Rakhal was sitting as if contemplating them. 'Are they rubies?'

'Diamonds,' Rakhal answered, and it was at that very moment she realised she was in serious trouble.

Oh, she had known it when she awoke on the plane, had known it too when she ran into the desert, but this was a different sort of trouble. When she saw the stones, and the care he was taking with his decision, she had a flutter in her stomach. Was he choosing a diamond for her? To be feeling like that was a very different sort of trouble indeed.

'There are also sapphires,' Rakhal said, and gestured for her to join him. 'It is a difficult decision. I do not want to cause offence.'

'Offence?'

'Diamonds are more valuable, especially pink ones, but here…'

He handed her two stones, both heavy and a purplish pink, and she held them up to the light, marvelling at the kaleidoscope that danced in them.

'They are beautiful, yes?'

'They're more than beautiful,' Natasha breathed, for it was as if an angel had chipped a piece out of heaven and dropped it to earth.

'The trouble is they are sapphires.'

'I thought sapphires were blue?'

She looked to him and he was smiling— a smile she had never seen, for it was black and unkind, but it was not aimed at her. He looked to the jewels she had put down.

'That I hope will be his first thought.'

'His?'

'King Emir of Alzan,' Rakhal said. 'I am to choose a gift to send to celebrate the gift of his twin girls. I first thought of diamonds—pink diamonds—but it is too obvious a choice, so I have had my people source the best in pink sapphires. I do not want to cause offence by giving a gift that is not valuable, but these are the best.' And then his smile darkened. 'But naturally when you think of sapphires you think of blue, and blue makes you think of sons.' Rakhal had made his choice. 'As Emir must be thinking…as the entire country is thinking…'

'Perhaps Emir is simply enjoying his gorgeous new girls.'

He looked at her and lay down on his cushions, and she lay down on hers, because sometimes, when neither was sulking, they talked. She'd told him about her family, about her parents and how she missed them so. About her job as a teacher. In turn he would tell her tales of the desert and sometimes, like this time, it was the only place on earth she wanted to be. His voice was rich and painted pictures in her mind, and tonight when he asked for the music to resume he told her she could remain.

'Generations ago the Sheikha Queen was to give birth in one full moon's time.' He smiled as she closed her eyes to the sound of his voice. He had never expected her to be so keen to learn of his land, had never known another who was not from here to be so interested in the tales of old. 'But the Queen surprised everyone. The birth was early, and they were expecting only one baby, but two sons were delivered. The *doula* was taken by surprise and there was confusion. With twins, the firstborn should be branded, to avoid any mistake, only these twins were a surprise, and they could not be sure who was the firstborn. Always there had been unrest in Alzanirz. The country was divided—'

'Why?' she interrupted. She looked over to him and saw that he was watching her, knew his eyes had been roaming her, and she loved the feeling of warmth.

'This side honoured the sky, the other the land. Both thought their way the most important. The King sought counsel and it was decided to appease all people. Each twin would rule half of the land.'

'So Emir and you are related?'

'Distantly.' Rakhal shrugged.

'And now he has twins?'

'He would have preferred sons,' Rakhal said. 'His wife was ill with this pregnancy— perhaps too ill to get pregnant again…'

'Poor thing.'

'It is good for Alzirz,' Rakhal explained. 'Perhaps Alzan will return to us soon.' He gave a wry smile. 'Emir has one brother, but he is not King material—he is too wild in his ways. Emir would never step aside for Hassan…and now he has two daughters! Twins divided us and now they will reunite us.'

She did not return his smile. 'Why would you want another country to rule over?'

'Why do you seek debate when there can be none? It was written many years ago. I don't expect you to understand.'

'I don't want to,' Natasha said. 'I cannot imagine being disappointed to have a daughter.'

'You do not have to,' Rakhal said. 'For here in Alzirz the sex of a child is not a concern. All the people want is healthy offspring and plenty of them.'

And she was stupid to have hoped he might be selecting a stone for *her*—even more stupid for thinking she wanted to be a part of this strange land. She stood and headed to her chambers.

'Where are you going?' He had been enjoying their talk.

'To my room.'

'You offend easily.'

'You so easily offend.'

He was tired of her moods, tired of her speaking back to him and yet he was not tired of *her.*

Rakhal summoned Abdul and asked that the sapphires be delivered to Emir in the morning. Pleased with his gift and the bile it would induce in his rival he headed to his sleeping quarters. But the brief pleasure died as he stretched out on the pillows and asked for the music to be silenced for he remembered the night she had shared his bed.

But perhaps he should ask the musician to resume, for his body craved a woman. So many times these past nights his hand had reached for the rope that would summon the mistress of his harem to send him a woman, and now, as he lay there, his mind awake and his body too, he thought of Natasha and what she might look like beneath the organza. He had only seen her covered, but he knew she would be hennaed and oiled, and though it was forbidden how he ached to taste and to see…

He ached…

His hand reached for the rope to pull it, so that he would not think of Natasha—for even if he wanted her he could not have her. If his child grew in her womb it should rest undisturbed.

He was hard at the thought of her. He should reach for the rope, not reach for himself, for that was also forbidden. There were twenty women who could attend to his needs tonight, except his mind craved only one.

'Rakhal?'

He had not heard her footsteps. It was only her voice that told him she had entered his quarters.

'You are not permitted here,' he barked, and rolled onto his side, but he knew that she had seen the rise of the silk.

'The music isn't playing, and anyway I can't sleep.'

She could not. Natasha knew from the ache low down in her stomach what the morning would bring—knew that it was their last real chance to be alone, that it might be their last chance to talk properly. Impossible as the rules were, Rakhal was not totally unreasonable. Unlike the night she had arrived, when she had felt so terrified and alone, now—despite their differences—there was a peace that only he brought, a smile that only he summoned, and never again would she fear him.

'I'm not tired.'

'Then pull your rope and one of the maids will bring you a potion—or give you a massage if you choose…'

'I want to talk.'

'Then I will have someone who speaks English come and read to you, or hold a conversation.'

'I meant to you,' Natasha answered. '*With* you.' When he said nothing she looked up. 'The stars are amazing tonight. Can they pull back my roof?'

'Tomorrow I will ask for it to be done.'

He wanted her gone, wanted to summon a woman from the harem. He did not want a circus parading in the tent tonight and fixing the roof when he wanted—no, *needed*—her gone. He felt the indent of the cushions and was appalled by her boldness as she sat down on the Prince's bed, where only the invited were allowed. He snapped on the light to scold her—and then wished that he hadn't for she looked amazing... her hair coiled over her shoulders and her mouth his for the taking. He must not.

'Go back to bed.'

'I'm not ten years old,' Natasha said. 'You can't just send me. I'm bored.'

'I am never bored.' He said it as an insult.

'Yes, well, you've got the best view. If I could look at the stars I wouldn't be bored either.' She lay down beside him but he moved away. 'I'm not here to seduce you.'

She grinned. There was nothing more beautiful than to lie on his bed and stare at the stars. And then her smile faded, for deep in her stomach she felt again a telltale cramp and moved her hand there. He watched, and was silent for a moment.

'You should sleep,' he said finally. 'Take the custards.'

But he knew somehow they were trying to hold back a tide that had turned. He could see the swell of her breasts and recalled the flash of tears tonight when another time she might have laughed. He did not want it to be tomorrow—did not want their time in the desert to end.

'I will show you the stars.'

He did. He called for gentle music and he showed her Orion, even if she could not make it out at first. It was like the best bed-time story, his deep, low voice telling her about the magnificent hunter and the red wound on his shoulder—the red star.

And she saw it.

'It is coming to the end of its life.'

'So what will happen to Orion?' She was tired now, but she loved his stories.

'He will burn brighter for a while,' Rakhal explained. 'When he explodes and dies he will burn so bright he will be visible in the daytime.'

'In our lifetime?'

'No.' He smiled.

'How soon?

'A million years.'

'And that's soon?'

'It is to the desert.'

He wanted to turn to her, wanted the tiny years of his life to shine with a significance that was alien to him. It was not about his title, it was about a significant other, and that did not mesh with one who would be King. His mind must marry only his country. He could ponder the sky no longer, and now he was restless.

But not Natasha. His voice and his stories had soothed her and maybe now she could sleep. She was growing rather fond of the custard. Maybe a drink would help her. Maybe the cramps would fade and she would have more time here. She would ask the maidens to bring her some of that sweet brew. He had told her she could ask for anything. Her fingers reached for the rope above his head and pulled it.

'What are you doing?' His hand snatched at hers, but too late.

'I want the potion,' she explained. 'I want something to help me sleep.'

And he tried.

Rakhal tried.

He told her to leave his bed, to go to her room, that the maids would bring it there. She could not understand his urgency, for he practically ordered her from the room, looked as if he was about to carry her. Then his voice stopped, and Natasha's head turned to the woman who was stepping in from the shadows. She could hear the jangle of jewels, see the outline of her scantily clad body and the veil over her face, and even as he ordered her away in his language, even when she had gone, the musky scent of her lingered, and Natasha thought she might vomit as realisation dawned.

'She was here to sleep with you.'

'No.'

'You were going to sleep with her tonight!' Her voice was rising. 'While I slept you were planning—'

'No!' It was Rakhal who shouted. '*You* were the one who summoned her.' He pointed to the rope. 'When you pulled that…'

And she laughed—a dangerous laugh, a furious laugh, an incredulous one. 'I pull mine and I bloody well get custard!'

'I did not pull it!' Rakhal shouted his defence. 'I have not.'

'But you can!'

She looked at him and there was guilt in his eyes, for tonight perhaps he might have.

'Yes.' His voice was a touch hoarse. 'Natasha, you must see reason. No man—no husband—will wait a year…'

'A *year*?'

'You would get three months to rest after having the baby.'

She loathed him, and she loathed this land.

With a sob she left the room.

She hated this place and its strange rules—hated what she might become. Hated that she would be served on a plate to him once a year. She could not win, could only lose. And she hated that her period was near, and the music simply added to her madness. She shouted for it to be silenced, but of course she was ignored. She shouted again as Rakhal, with a sash at his hips, dashed from his room. He called for the maidens, for Natasha was raging, and they took her to her room, tried to force a drink on her and not the one she knew. But her screams grew louder. She screamed as if she was being poisoned.

Finally Rakhal intervened and took the brew from the maids.

'This is cucumber to clear your head, and chestnut to calm you, and there is wild garlic too, to calm the anger…'

'You're poisoning me!' she shouted. 'You're sedating me so you can sleep with her.'

'Are you mad?' Rakhal demanded. 'Are you mad enough to think I would give you something that would harm—?'

'Am I going mad?' she begged. She truly thought she was, because she knew then that she loved him, and all he wanted from her was a baby. And she hated the harem, and that he had shared himself with the women there. 'I can't bear to be here for another minute.'

'You must sleep.'

'I can't sleep with them watching.'

'Leave,' he said to his maidens, and when she still would not calm he took her kicking and screaming and carried her to his bed.

'I have not slept with anyone since you!' he roared, and he cursed, for it was killing him that he hadn't. But still she did not calm, so he picked up his scythe. She screamed as he raised it and then he sliced the rope. *There!*

And she stopped, but her breathing was heavy. The sheer organza robe had risen and he tried not to look.

'I have not slept with anyone,' he said,

and his breathing was hard too. He stood over where she lay.

'And yet you won't sleep with me?'

'No,' Rakhal said.

But he watched her gold curls disappear as she covered herself with the organza and she saw his eyes linger, saw the set of his jaw as he resisted what was normal.

She had only this chance and she took it. 'You don't have to treat me like glass, Rakhal.'

Still his eyes roamed.

'What did the maidens do?' He was curious when he should not be.

'They painted me.'

He should not know of these things, but he knew a little, and his eyes flicked to her breasts. They were two tempting peaks, the nipples jutting, and he had to hold in his tongue so as not to lick one. Her body was pink beneath the sheer fabric and he knew where they would have painted her. So badly he wanted to see, to peel back the organza and explore her body, to see what a royal prince never should.

Her voice spoke on. 'I'm bored waiting for my period, I'm bored being treated like glass, and it kills me being with you and you not touching me.'

Still he did nothing. She moaned in frustration, and he sensed danger as she climbed from the bed.

'Where are you going?'

'To bed.'

'For your hands to roam your body?' He could see the lust in her eyes.

'Well, yours won't.'

'It is forbidden…'

'For you, perhaps,' Natasha said. 'What are you going to do? Tie me to the bed?'

'It could be bad for the baby.'

'Oh, please.' She could not stand it, could not bear it. She put her hands to her ears. 'La-la-la…' She would not give in to his thinking. 'You don't know what you're missing. Pregnancy is beautiful, and your wife's body would crave you, and instead you'd be with *her.*'

She jabbed at the torn rope; she was going insane in the desert, but it wasn't just sex, it was him. It was his caress that she craved, his mouth where there was heat, and she wanted his mind and his days and his nights too.

And perhaps Natasha had driven him crazy too, for he turned from the rules and to her.

He must not make love to her, but he could kiss her.

He pushed her down onto the bed. He would take the edge off her burning desire.

He hushed her with his mouth and she caved in to his tongue. But his words took the pleasure away.

'Just a kiss,' he said.

'No.'

For he'd made it worse. His touch had made it more, not less, and she climbed from his bed and went to her own.

He stared to the skies for an answer, to the shapes and the stories he knew well. There was not a jewel on the earth that matched a single star's splendour, but not even the stars could tell him what to do.

CHAPTER FOURTEEN

NATASHA awoke to the sound of him pray-
ing and knew he would not change—perhaps she had no right to expect him to.
They were from different worlds after all .

She walked out to the breakfast table,
but did not sit down on the floor to wait
for him to join her; instead she went to the
wash area to have what she already knew
confirmed.

The maidens bowed their heads as she
informed them, and then she walked back
to her bedroom and dressed in the clothes
she had arrived in. As she pulled on her un-
derwear she saw the fading flowers low on
her stomach and ached with a strange grief
that they would not blossom and grow and
stretch. She mourned for something that
had never been, nor could ever be.

Rakhal was seated on the floor at the

breakfast table and turned when he heard her approach. His smile faded when he saw her face and registered the maidens who were quietly weeping, for they had grown fond of Natasha.

He dismissed them, and she was relieved that he did so, for she could not stand their tears. It was her period, for God's sake, Natasha reasoned, not a baby she had lost. But her own disappointment sideswiped her. Might she crave what once she had feared?

'It wasn't meant to be.' Rakhal's voice was practical, though he cursed his own restraint, berated not taking her that second night—for then they would have had the ways of old on their side. 'You must be relieved?'

'Of course,' she lied, 'and so must you…' She attempted a smile but her lips would not move.

'No.' He stood, for he did not want it to be over. 'I should be relieved.' And he did what he did not usually do—or never had till he had met her. He wrapped her in his arms and attempted to comfort her. 'But I am not.'

And she did something that no one had

ever tried to do with him, for he had never needed it: the arms that coiled around his neck offered comfort to *him*.

She let the tears fall and he held her, and they mourned what had never existed, let go of what could never be.

'You can return to your life,' Rakhal said.

'You can choose your bride.'

And he felt her arms around him and offered what he'd thought he never would. But he wanted her in his life. He would somehow deal with his father's disapproval and the fear and anger from his people at such an unwise choice—more so than if she were already pregnant.

'I choose you.' Rakhal bestowed the greatest honour. 'I choose you to be my wife. I will marry you in fourteen days and you can come to my bed again.'

'Only to be removed from it two days later,' Natasha said, her eyes spilling tears as she looked up at him. 'Only to be taken away when I'm pregnant and then brought back a year later.'

'That is how it is,' Rakhal said. 'That is how it must be.'

'And the harem?'

'This is our way.'

'But it's not mine!' She tried to fathom it, tried to see herself as a part of it, but then shook her head and declined his proposal. 'No, I will not be your wife.'

'It is overwhelming, I know.' He did not linger on her refusal. In a moment she would come around. 'I will deal with my father; in time the people will accept—'

'It's not your father or the people I need to accept me.' Natasha looked at him. 'It's you, Rakhal, and you won't. So, no, I won't marry you.'

'Have you any idea of the honour I'm giving you by asking?' His arms released her.

She missed the shield of them and yet she stood firm, looked at his incredulous face and was angry for both of them. Angry that he simply did not get it—that he could not see how lonely his idea of a marriage would make her.

'Have you any idea of my shame that you did?'

'Shame?'

'Yes—shame!' Natasha was not crying

now. Her eyes glittered instead with fury, and some of it was inward for she was so very tempted to say yes. But at what cost? she reminded herself as she spoke to him, as she pictured the future she simply must deny. 'To be *brought* to your bed to provide you and your country with children. To know that when the need arises you simply pull a rope… I want a partner, Rakhal— I want someone to share my life with, the good bits and the bad, someone who wants *me*, not just the babies I can give him. It's not going to happen, Rakhal. I want my passport. I want to go home.'

'Your Highness…' Abdul walked in at the most painful of moments.

'Not now!' Rakhal roared.

But Abdul did not flee. He stood and spoke to Rakhal in their own language and Natasha watched as Rakhal's face paled. He gave a brief nod and uttered a response, then turned to her.

'Abdul has just delivered some serious news.'

'Your father?'

Rakhal shook his head. 'No, but I do need to speak with him. You will wait here.'

And she waited for what was close to an hour until he returned. She'd hoped they would speak now more calmly, but Rakhal had other things on his mind.

'I have to leave,' Rakhal said. 'I need to leave on this helicopter. But my people will arrange transport for you—whatever you want—if you choose to stay in a hotel for a few days, or see your brother, or...' He hesitated. So badly he wanted to ask that she stay, but so badly it burned that she had refused him.

'Rakhal—' She was angry with him, but Natasha understood that something might have happened to his father. Yet he was dismissing her so coolly just because her period had come, just because she would not accept his ways, and that was the last straw. 'You really know how to make a woman feel used.'

'I asked you to be my bride less than an hour ago,' Rakhal said, 'and yet you accuse me of making you feel used.' He did not have time for another row, and neither did he have time to explain properly, but he tried. 'Emir...' Rakhal's words were sparse. 'His wife died at dawn.'

'The twins' mother…?'

He gave a brief nod. 'I must attend the burial, offer him condolences.'

'Of course.'

And then Abdul came, and he must have informed Rakhal that his transport was ready for he nodded and said to Natasha that he must now leave. Abdul said something else, more words that she did not understand, but they were said with a smile that had Natasha's stomach churning.

'What did Abdul just say?' she challenged when he had gone.

'Nothing.'

'Is this good news for Alzirz?' She would not relent. 'Has it bought you some time?'

'They were his words, not mine,' Rakhal pointed out. 'Yes, it gives us some time. But for now…' He felt as if a mirror was cracking in his mind. 'Now Emir will be deeply grieving. In Alzan…' how he wished she could understand '…because the King can take another wife they live as you would choose.'

And it was as if he was back in London, staring out of the window. The blackness in his soul had returned—only he recognised it this time. Recognised the jealousy that had burnt there. For in Alzan, where there could be more than one partner in a lifetime, all hope for the country's future was not pinned on one bride. There the royals could live and love together and watch their family grow.

'So could you,' Natasha said, when he'd tried to explain to her.

Rakhal shook his head, for it could not be. 'The people would never accept it. The King can be married only to his country. The wife of the King is to be—'

'Locked away!' Natasha shouted. 'Kept on a luxurious shelf and taken down when needed!' She hated Alzirz, hated this land and its strange ways, except she loved *him*. 'Please, can you just think about it? Even if not for me. If you do marry a more suitable woman, can you at least think about it for *her*?'

'I have to leave.' There was no time to argue and Rakhal knew there was no point either. Had Natasha been pregnant there would have been no discussion—she would have had to conform to their ways—but she was not, so why didn't he feel relief?

He should just go, and he moved to do so—did not give her a kiss. She had refused his offer and so it was not his place. But still he could not end it.

'Stay.' He swallowed his pride and forced the word. 'We can speak on my return…'

'And you'll think about it?'

He gave a nod, for how could he not think about it? And yet it was an impossible ask. The King's mind must be only on his country, not on his children or his wife.

As he boarded the helicopter and it lurched into the sky, so too did his stomach lurch as Abdul made another comment about Emir that a few weeks ago might have brought a wry smile to Rakhal's lips.

Today it did not.

'You will show respect.' He stared at his aide.

'I would not say it to *him*.'

'And neither should you say it to me.'

He saw the set of his aide's chin, saw the pursing of his lips, for the Prince was more than chastising him. He was turning his back on a rivalry of old and it would no doubt be reported to the King. But his time with Natasha had changed things.

This morning he had woken with a woman in his bed and hope for the future—he had glimpsed how Emir had lived.

And he wanted it.

Even the grief…

Such grief on Emir's features as Rakhal entered the Palace of Alzan and he kissed him on both cheeks, as was their way. He offered him his sympathy, as was their way too; only for Rakhal it felt different. This time Rakhal spoke from a place he never had before. His words came from his heart.

Not that Emir noticed.

An English nanny held the tiny twins and she was weeping when Rakhal went over. He kissed each twin's tiny cheek and offered them too his condolences. The babies were teary and fretful, and a veiled woman apologised to Rakhal.

'They miss their mother's milk.'

He did not nod and return to the men; instead he lifted one tiny child, whose name, he was informed, was Clemira, and told the veiled woman that it was her mother she missed. In that moment he missed his own.

Pink sapphires did not seem such a suitable gift now.

And the Sheikha Queen, Rakhal realised, was in fact indispensable. For he looked at Emir and realised he had loved his wife. Now Emir would have the agony of finding another bride while still grieving his loss.

As might he.

CHAPTER FIFTEEN

'You have been granted full privileges.'

She wanted Rakhal, but instead it was Abdul who returned that night and told her of her *reward*—that she could travel freely to visit her brother, go to the desert or to the harem and perhaps surprise Rakhal. Rakhal would see her at times in London too.

The meaning and intent were clear, and Natasha glimpsed her future—a life that was a little more taken care of, for he had paid funds for her time here that were generous, and her brother's debts were sorted out. She could return to Alzirz when she chose—except it would kill her.

To have the man she loved as an occasional treat, a reward for them both now and then with no strings, an exotic fantasy she could return to at times…

For how long? Natasha thought with tears in her eyes.

Till the time when her body was no longer the one he wanted? When she did not amuse him any more?

'Rakhal knows that I would never agree to this.' She shook her head. 'I want to speak to him.'

'Prince Rakhal wants to concentrate now on duty,' Abdul explained. 'I have arranged transport to take you back to London.'

'No.' He had asked her to stay till he returned and she did not believe Abdul. 'I want to see him.'

'It is not about *your* wants,' Abdul said. 'And Prince Rakhal knows that, which is why he has placed this stamp.'

She looked at the passport he handed to her. On it was the gold stamp that Abdul could not fake, for it could only come from Rakhal. What hurt her the most was not his coarse offer, but the fact that she considered it in the knowledge that somehow her body was now forever his. Somehow so too was her heart, even if she must leave. After Rakhal no one else would ever suffice.

'I must return to the Prince now. A helicopter will take you to the airport.'

She lay alone on his bed and waited for
the transport that would prise her away
from the desert she loved and the rules
that she loathed. She wanted to speak with
him just one more time—wanted Rakhal to
look her in the eye and tell her it was over.

She could hear the laughter and noises of
the harem, the splashes in the pool and the
music that seduced. She begged the stars
for an answer, but all they did was shine silver—except one that was maybe a planet.
That one shone a little gold, as she had on
the night she had met him, and as her heart
shone now with hope.

'You should not be here.' The madam
scolded her as she parted the curtain. 'You
should not wander.'

But she showed the madam the gold
stamp and with that she could not argue.

'It will be at a time of my choosing,
though,' the madam warned her. 'You will
not be called on for now. When he returns
from the funeral the Prince will be in deep
tahir, but that will change before the wedding.'

And the gold stamp gave her rare status, for when a furious Abdul came to the tent late in the night, to insist that she take her flight to London, the madam shooed him away—for here the madam ruled.

She learnt so much in those days—the harem was nothing like she'd imagined. The women there were spoiled and pampered too. They were massaged and oiled and kept beautiful, and they spent their time chatting and laughing, reading and swimming, as any group of girlfriends on a luxury holiday together would.

'We are spoiled by the Prince,' said Nadia, who had a throaty French accent.

Natasha had been surprised to find out that not all the women were from Alzirz. The Prince, it would seem, liked variety.

'Before I came here,' explained Calah, who was from Alzirz, 'my family was poor and I was to be married to an old man— to keep his home and share his filthy bed. I ran away, and I would have been working the streets, but I was lucky and I was chosen. Now I live in luxury and my family is being taken care of. I am studying

for a degree—' she smiled at Natasha
'—and sometimes I get to be with the
Prince.' Her eyes challenged the doubt in
Natasha's. 'Which is always a pleasure.'

Natasha's cheeks burnt as she heard the
other women discuss him, and she dreaded
the ring of the bell that, for Natasha, would
sound the end if the madam did not first
choose her.

But days passed and the bell did not
ring—and then Natasha found out why. 'He
is meeting with the King,' the madam explained. 'Soon his bride will be announced.
Tomorrow, they say.' She smiled to her
girls and all but Natasha returned it. 'Our
Prince will announce his bride.'

CHAPTER SIXTEEN

RAKHAL stared out of the palace windows
to the celebrations that were starting in the
street.

'It is good to see the people so happy,'
the King said. 'They fear my passing, they
know now that it will be soon, and the wedding will please them.'

'The people have nothing to fear,' Rakhal
said. 'I will be a good leader.'

He would be. He had visions for his
country and he knew that the people were
ready. The wealth from the mines needed
to be better returned to the people; infra-
structure was needed—hospitals, schools
and universities. But at a pace that would
do no harm. His heart told him to protect
the desert, not to inflict upon it modern
ways—and he needed a clear head for that.
He needed time alone and deep reflection

for every decision he would make—not a wife who would demand he speak to her, who would pout when she was bored. Yet at that moment his heart ached for the same.

'I have just days,' the King said. 'Soon the people will be in mourning. You must change that. You must give them an heir, give them hope…'

Rakhal looked out to the sea of people and thought of the grief that would soon seep into them. He knew his plans for the future would scare them rather than please. Theirs would be a grief that only a bride and a baby would appease.

But the bride he wanted could not be found—his people were still searching for her. She was back in London, Abdul had informed him, and yet she would not take his calls.

Rakhal had not thought it possible to mourn a living person, yet it felt as if he did, and he mourned too a baby that had never existed. He did not understand how Natasha could leave without speaking with him.

'If I fly to London—'

'Enough!' The King was furious with

his son—furious that still Rakhal insisted on bringing up this Natasha—and he let his displeasure show. 'Still—even as death creeps in—you try to postpone your duty.'

'I do not want to postpone it—I accept that I must marry. But if I could just speak to her…'

'And say what?' the King demanded. 'That you bend to her whims instead of serving your people? *Never.*' The King had had enough. 'Now we will feast, but tomorrow you will step onto the balcony wearing the gold braid and let the people know you have chosen your wife.'

Rakhal frowned, for this was straying from tradition .

'Tomorrow I will step onto the balcony wearing the gold braid, but now I return to the desert,' Rakhal said. 'And I will feast and celebrate there, and tomorrow I will return and choose from your selection.'

'Better you are here,' the King snapped. 'Save your seed for your bride.'

'I'm sure,' Rakhal snapped back, 'that there is plenty.'

And he did not bend to his father—not even now; instead he returned to the desert, and then to the land his mother had once roamed. He roamed it now with his eagle.

Since Natasha had left he had not shaved nor bathed.

He prayed and he sat and he tried to meditate.

A dust devil formed and he heard his mother laugh at his problems. She did not understand that tomorrow he must announce a wife, that the people would panic if it did not happen. She laughed and she danced and he did not understand.

He felt the sun on his skull and tried to clear his thoughts, to let them slip out of his mind as fast as they came in, to clear his head so he might be centred.

He did this often.

Rakhal would clear his head and let the silent desert fill it, let the voice of the wind and the stories in the sand infuse him. He trusted in the answers. But no matter how long he sat, no matter how he tried to empty his mind, to focus on his country and the leadership that would soon be his, all too soon Natasha would fill his thoughts.

He could not speak to his aides, nor his family—for they would not give unbiased counsel. They would not contemplate let alone discuss changes to the monarchy, to the rules and their ways; they would never permit his thinking. His grandfather had taught a young Rakhal the desert ways, though, and even if his son had rejected them his grandson had not.

He loved the desert as he loved the stars, sought wisdom from the dunes, and he knew then what he must do.

He took his eagle and let it circle.

And then he sent his eagle to the skies again.

If he did it a third time the Bedouins would be alerted.

If he did it a fourth they would continue with their day.

But if the bird ceased flying after three times the wizened old man would be summoned.

Rakhal sought his counsel rarely, though it was rumoured that Emir, at times, met with the old man too.

Within the hour Rakhal sat with a man who had seen one hundred and twenty yellow moons and heard again about two tests. And Rakhal silently questioned why he would ask someone so old about ways that should be new.

'I need to think of my country,' Rakhal said, 'except I think of her. I need my mind to be clear of her.'

'I will guide you in meditation,' the old man said.

Rakhal sat and let his mind empty, but still it was Natasha's face that he saw.

'Take your mind to the stars and beyond them.'

Rakhal did. But still she was there.

The old man took him further, past Orion, beyond the planets, and still there she was.

'To the edge of the universe,' the old man said.

But still she was there.

'To the end of the universe.'

She was there waiting.

'And beyond the end,' the old man instructed.

But there she was.

'And beyond the end again.'

Her image was not fading.

'It does not end.' Rakhal opened his eyes to the old man and hissed his frustration.

'It cannot end,' the old man said, and stood. 'Trust the desert. Trust in the traditions and the ways of old.'

'She doesn't want the ways of old.'

'Tonight you should trust in them.'

But the ways of old were not being adhered to.

Rakhal returned to his tent and declined a feast of fruit and music to please him. He watched as the arak turned white when Abdul added ice, and he turned down the hookah—all the traditional ways for a prince to behave before he made his choice.

'I wish to bathe.'

He summoned the maidens and asked that Abdul leave, for tonight he would be busy and the arak and the hookah would not help with that.

He laughed and chatted with the maidens who bathed him, and lay back as he was shaved, and then he rose from the bath, dressed in as little as was expected. And still Abdul remained.

'You will leave,' Rakhal said, and instructed the musician to play a more suitable choice for his mood.

'Drink.' Again Abdul pushed a glass towards him. 'Celebrate these last hours of freedom.'

And Rakhal was certain now that she was near.

CHAPTER SEVENTEEN

'HE HAS bathed!' The madam clapped her hands and got her girls' attention. 'And he has shaved, and he has summoned music and the most potent of foods....'

Her voice trailed off as Abdul appeared, and Natasha watched the madam's eyes narrow as he whispered some words.

They all waited but the bell did not ring, and she held her breath in hope, for maybe Rakhal could change even if not for her. But then came the kick in the guts of disappointment when finally it rang, and she could picture his hand reaching out to the rope on the bed where they had lain. There was a flurry of activity, the girls rubbing in oils and teasing their hair, doing their make-up and chattering excitedly as they tried to guess who might be chosen. Natasha held her breath and prayed it would be her.

'Nadia.'

The madam slipped a *yashmak* over the scantily dressed woman and sprayed her with a musky scent. It filled Natasha's nostrils and she felt like retching, for it was the same scent that had entered their room that night.

'It has been a while. His need will be great.'

The madam gave Nadia instructions and as she disappeared into the night Natasha lay on the cushions, closing her eyes against tears, trying and failing not to imagine what they were doing. She felt pure loss as their time together was terminated by a single ring of the bell, as her prince returned to the ways he knew best.

And her last tiny glimmer of hope died—a foolish hope, a stupid hope, she thought—when Nadia returned just fifteen minutes later.

'Leave Nadia,' the madam scolded as all the women except Natasha gathered around Nadia to ask how the Prince was. 'She will bathe and get some rest.'

But the madam frowned as Nadia went to her cushions and lay silent. The other girls frowned too, for usually there was a more excited return.

Over and over he shamed her.

The bell rang through the night, and Natasha screwed her eyes closed as one by one the women returned and he made a mockery of all they had been, all she had asked him to consider. Finally, when the bell was quiet, when the women all dozed and slept, she prayed for sunlight. Dawn would be here soon. He would go to prayer and she would leave, Natasha decided. At first light she would leave.

And then the bell rang.

The madam stood and parted the curtain, looked outside and then over to Natasha. She put her fingers to her lips and summoned her.

Natasha was draped in a small skirt with a tiny coined fringe and beneath it she was naked. Her breasts were dressed with the same noisy fabric too, and a veil was placed to just reveal her eyes. She was told what it would mean should he gesture that she remove the veil. If he did that she would

slap his face instead, Natasha decided. As
the madam came to her with the musk Natasha shook her head, again remembering
that night one of the women had come to
the room. The scent still made her ill, but
the madam insisted.

'He will be sleepy,' the mistress explained,
'so you may not get to surprise him.'

Surprise him? Natasha thought darkly.
She'd more likely spit at him—not that
she would tell the madam that; instead she
stood as she was delivered more instructions.

'He might not want any conversation.
Do your duty silently with him, so that the
Prince's mind can wander where it chooses.
Let his hand guide you and if he talks just
say you speak English,' the madam said.
'But rarely does he speak. Prince Rakhal
does not waste time with conversation.'

She put a gold bangle on Natasha's wrist,
and large earrings in her ears that fell in
gold rows—because, the madam said, he
liked the noise. Natasha hated finding that
out from another woman.

And then it was on with a *yashmak*.

As she left the tent the madam again put

a finger to her lips, for outside lay a sleeping Abdul. There was a flutter of hope in Natasha's stomach, a hope she dared not examine, for she understood Abdul's instructions were that she be kept from him.

The madam hurried Natasha through to his tent, and as they got there the madam paused. 'He deserves happiness,' she said, and there were tears in her eyes as she kissed Natasha on the cheek.

She was left alone to enter—there were no maidens guarding his shadow tonight—and she could see his profile on the bed. In a moment she would face him.

Or rather, Natasha thought, holding her head high, Rakhal would face *her*.

CHAPTER EIGHTEEN

STILL her phone was not answered, and Rakhal lay back on the bed and knew he was foolish even to hope.

All night he had hoped she would come to him—had done as he'd been told and trusted in the ways of old—had stupidly almost convinced himself that his father and Abdul were keeping the harem from him for a reason.

Soon the morning would be here. He would pray and then head to the palace, and there could be no more putting it off. Today he would announce his bride, and from there there could be no turning back.

He heard soft footsteps and then the jangle of jewellery, and as the woman entered and the heavy scent of musk reached Rakhal the last vestige of hope died. For he knew she did not like jewellery or scent. He also knew in his heart that Natasha would never join the harem—it had been but a pipe dream.

The room was dark and the music played louder as Natasha stepped into his abode. Nervously she stood for a moment, looked to where he lay on the bed naked, a silk drape over his groin. He did not look up as she walked towards him. He did not look over, but spoke in Arabic to her.

She did not answer. Her throat was dry, and she was terrified that he would recognise her, that he would be furious. She walked slowly to the bed, reaching out her hand to him, to speak with him, to explain that she was here finally to talk. But what was the point? Natasha thought bitterly. She felt cheated on after the past night.

'Did you not understand what I said?' His hand grabbed hers as she reached out to touch him. 'I said that you are to take the jewel that is on the table.'

She did *not* understand—although he had spoken in English this time. The madam had said nothing of this. Perhaps he meant afterwards, Natasha thought, and when his grip released her hand she hovered over his stomach. She saw the snake of hair that had teased her the day they had met. Rather than a row or a confrontation, she wanted one last time with him before the magic must end, and her finger moved to lightly trace the hair. She watched as his stomach tightened.

'Take the jewel,' he said, 'and never speak of this to anyone. Go now and sit on that chair for a suitable time.' The musky scent filled his nostrils, the sound of her bangles jangled, and all he wanted was Natasha. 'If you talk, even amongst the others, I will know. You are to take the jewel as payment for your silence. My mind is with another. I need to think.'

Except his body betrayed him, for still those fingers traced the hair on his lower stomach. He grew hard even as he resisted, and the silk slithered away. Still the finger explored the flat plane of his stomach, and it was as if his skin recognised her. So light was her touch that it could have been Natasha's—but he halted her there, his fingers lingering with regret on the bangles that had tainted his fantasy that it was her. She released him—but only to take the bangles off.

'Take the jewel and leave.' He was close to begging as her hand returned, yet he did not halt it, for the hand that now held him was silent, and it allowed him to remember. 'Take the jewel,' he said, as he had to the other girls throughout the night. He had hoped so badly to find Natasha, but now his body gave in.

She watched, fascinated, watched him rise and grow at such a slight touch. It was as if his body welcomed her back even as he tried to douse it.

'My mind is with another.'

'I can be her,' she whispered, for she knew it was *her* that he was thinking of, and she smiled at what he had done.

She understood now Nadia and the other girls' silence when they had returned. He had kept himself unto her, and though his hand was tight over her wrist she moved her other hand over the magnificence that was waiting, stroked a finger lightly along it.

'You can think of her...' She took the hand that gripped her to her breast, felt his hand flat and resisting against it, then a reluctant exploration as still she stroked him.

'Take the jewel.' His teeth were gritted, for his mind was playing tricks. Beneath the musk he could smell her delicious fresh scent, and he did not want to open his eyes and be disappointed all over again—did not want to taint the fantasy that it was her. Was this what he was destined to do for the rest of his life? To close his eyes and imagine it was her?

Yes, Rakhal realised, for she could not be found.

'Please...' he begged this wanton woman who should follow orders.

But without order she had removed her veil. Her lips were at his tip now, and he could feel her hair on his stomach. He curled his fingers into her hair to lift her head, to tell her to stop, but there was a devil that begged him let her work on, for her mouth was a soothing balm and her tongue knew just what to do in a way others did not.

'Let me be her.' Natasha smiled and licked him, licked his delicious length, and then took in the moist tip and slowly caressed it. She berated the sound of her earrings, for they had distracted him, and could only admire his roar of restraint as he yanked at her hair and pulled her head back, almost weeping to the dark.

'I love another!'

How angrily he said it, but how delicious it was to hear it.

'Then let me love *you*,' she said, taking her earrings out as she returned her mouth to him.

'I am to share my bed only with her. My people are searching for her now,' Rakhal said. But her mouth was back and he was weak.

He must get rid of this woman who had crept into his head, who knew what he liked, who made him weak, made a strong man give in. He reached for the lamp, for he must end this fantasy, yet as he turned on the light there were red curls cascading over him and it killed him not to come. There was white pale skin and it was a cruel torture to be tested like this.

He lifted her head and saw her eyes and it was Natasha—or was his mind playing tricks? Could he convince himself so fully as he made love with another that it was her?

'Natasha…' And there beneath the make up and musk it was surely her. 'I have been searching…'

'I've been here.' There was hurt in her eyes. 'Your gold seal assured me access to all areas.'

Ardour was replaced by anger as realisation dawned. 'I did not grant that…'

'Only you can.'

'Or the King.' He knew the lengths his people would go to, to keep traditions safe, but that his father would take such an active part in it—would do anything to keep the ways of old—etched a new river of pain. 'They were not even looking for you.'

'Abdul knew where I was,' Natasha explained. 'He's outside guarding the harem now—or supposed to be.'

Anger propelled him from the bed. He pulled on a sash, scanned the room for his robe. He would go to Abdul first, kill him with his bare hands so blind was he with fury.

'He fell asleep. I think he thought you were done for the night.'

He heard the tremble of rage in her voice and knew he would deal with Abdul later. There was something more important to address than his aide.

'I paid them a jewel for their silence,' Rakhal said. 'I could not think of being with another since I have been with you.'

'But one day you might. When I am away being *pampered*, or when we've had a row and I haven't agreed with something you said, or when I'm old or sick…'

She looked to the rope and she loathed it, but his eyes did not wander there; instead he looked at the woman he had missed every night they had been apart. He never wanted to sleep alone again— which sounded a lot like the love she insisted upon.

'No.' He shook his head. 'Those ways are over.'

'You say that now.'

He meant it. For here was the one living person who did not care about his title, who did not care for his luxuries, did not care about the prestige that marrying him would bring. All she wanted was *him*, and it was humbling indeed to look love in the eye and recognise it.

So he *asked* her for the first time, when before he had bestowed an honour. 'Will you be my wife?'

And Natasha stood there silent—because if she opened her mouth she'd say yes, would settle for two nights a month knowing that he loved her.

But her silence forced him to continue.

'Will you share in my life?' Rakhal asked. 'All of it?'

'The people…' She could not take it in. 'The traditions…'

'The people want a strong ruler,' Rakhal said. 'And I will be stronger with you by my side. In time they will come to understand.'

He pulled her towards him. He saw her as if for the first time. He traced her lips with his fingers to be sure, and then he tasted them again to prove it to himself. And he dipped his sash in the water by his bed and washed off the musk, took off the clothes she had worn for him. He wanted only her now, and he kissed her till she was writhing, till their bodies were locked deep in their own rhythm and her neck arched back and her mouth moaned. The music heightened and their bodies moved in the shadows above.

There would be changes, she thought faintly, but for tonight she would celebrate the ways of the desert and the music that was made for them.

'I can spend the rest of my life making love to you.' How could he have thought it was a concession? This was heaven he had found. She was a part of him and he could love her for ever.

He imagined her heavy with his child, those breasts full and milky. He would love every change in her. He would witness each one.

She was over and on top of him; she made love to him as he had once made love to her; she gave in to him completely, taken to a new place, to a future that would be different. And she did not fear it, for Rakhal would be walking with her.

She felt the tremble of her orgasm and there was no halting it. The music urged them on and, unsheathed, he spilled inside her, for they never needed to hold back from each other again.

'We marry soon.'

He held her as he told her, and she did not resist, for she wanted that too.

'The people will hear today that my bride has been chosen.' He wanted more than that for Natasha, though—wanted the changes to start this very day. 'Today they will *see* who I have chosen. I will return to the palace with you by my side. You will step out on the balcony with me.'

And later she was taken and bathed. The maidens knew the secret, for perhaps she might be with child, and this time when she was oiled and hennaed she knew she would be returned to him. She even had a little joke with Amira, for she was not wearing her mother's jewels.

'I will fetch them for you,' Amira said, and it felt nice to wear them on this day as pretty flowers were painted over her womb. So badly she wanted to see them grow.

Rakhal too was bathed, and dressed in a robe of black. His *kafiya* should be tied with a silver braid till his selection, but it was already decorated with a braid of gold, for the choice had already been made—by both of them.

Natasha was nervous as she sat for the second time in a helicopter—though not so terrified as she had been the first time. Rakhal sat beside her and she looked down at her hand in his, saw the long fingers and manicured nails and felt the warmth of his skin around hers. She glanced over to Abdul, who sat sweating and pale opposite them—for Rakhal had not yet said a word to his aide.

And Natasha said nothing either, as she sat in a lounge with the maidens and Abdul went in with Rakhal to address his father.

She waited for shouts, for protests, for rage. But the walls must be thick, for all she heard was the low murmur of Rakhal's deep voice, and then the door opened and as always he made her heart hammer. As on the first day, a blush rose in her cheeks and she fought the urge to run to him.

'What did he say?'

'That he does not consent. That the wedding cannot go ahead without his blessing,' Rakhal said.

She felt her stomach tighten in dread, felt the weight of tradition force them apart, but Rakhal gave a dismissive shrug to his father's threats.

'I told him that I did not need his blessing. That I will show my bride to the people today and we will marry when I rule, if that is how my father chooses to be.'

She had not met the King, had only heard of his power and might, but today no might could match Rakhal's, for his eyes were as dark as the night sky, his stance resolute, and it was clear he would not be deterred.

'I told him I have learnt not just from our teachings but from our mistakes—from *his* mistakes, from his regret at not having my mother by his side.'

She could hear Abdul weeping beside her.

'For years he has mourned her. He could have been with her. She pined not for the desert but for him.'

Rakhal closed his eyes for a brief moment, dragged in air, and she could only imagine how hard it must have been to say it, let alone for the King to hear it.

'I have learnt from his mistakes and I

choose to do things differently. Or else…'
He looked at his soon-to-be bride but did
not continue.

Natasha now spoke for him. 'You would
never walk away from your people.'

'Of course not,' Rakhal said. 'My people trust me to make the right decision and
they will not turn away from me.'

But a muscle flickered in his cheek as
he said that, and Natasha was not so sure.

'We must greet the people now,' he said.

They walked up a vast staircase. She
could hear shouts and cheers from the
people outside, waiting for their Prince
to come out, and she was terribly, terribly nervous—especially when the maidens took off her robe and arranged her hair.
She looked to Rakhal, who was also being
readied, a sash placed around his shoulders,
his *kafiya* already roped in gold. He stood
tall and strong, ready to face the judgement
of his people.

'Whatever their response,' Rakhal said,
'know that I am proud.'

She could not do this to him—to the
people, to the King. But Rakhal silenced
her protests and ordered the balcony doors

open. He took her hand and stepped out to face the crowd.

The noise was deafening, and the silence, as the shouts faded, was deafening too. They saw their Prince with his chosen bride and there were gasps of bewilderment as they realised she stood by his side. Her hair was blowing in the breeze and his hand gripped hers tighter.

And then she heard a cough behind her, turned. For the first time Natasha met the King—a thinner, older version of Rakhal, his face etched with the pain of half a lifetime buried in regret. Her heart could not fail to love him—especially when he stepped forward and took her other hand and then raised it to the crowd. The cheering resumed, with claps and the shouts from the people, as the King blessed his son's choice.

A few days later she was draped in gold, as she had been the night he found her, and led to him. She curtsied to the King and smiled at her proud brother.

They were married in the gardens of the palace, then driven through the streets—

and the people cheered for them, for there had always been a sadness in the Sheikh Crown Prince's eyes and it was gone now. They had mourned the passing of his mother and seen the happiness die in their King's eyes, but now love had returned to Alzirz and now they cheered for it.

For the love their Prince had found with his bride.

EPILOGUE

THE King was returned to the desert just before sunset. He had lasted another three months but death, when it came, was swift, and that morning they had been urgently summoned to farewell him.

One by one they went to him, even King Emir of Alzan and the tiny princesses. For though there was rivalry, there were deep traditions too. And after Natasha had been in to see him she sat with Amy, the nanny, because she was English too.

'How are they?' The girls were gorgeous, with big black eyes that were as solemn as the day.

'They're doing well.' Amy gave a tight smile.

'And King Emir?'

'I don't know,' Amy said. 'We don't really see him.' She looked down at the babies, and there was a wry note to her voice and a flash of tears in her eyes as she addressed them. 'Do we, girls?'

'But…' It was not her place to question, but Rakhal had told her that it was different in Alzan, that the royals raised their own children. Clearly this wasn't the case. Natasha looked over as Emir came out from his time with the King, but he did not glance over to his girls; instead he sat in quiet prayer.

And then it was Rakhal's time to go in, and there he remained with his father till the end.

Today they stood where the palace gave way to the desert, and there was wailing and tears, but Rakhal stood stoic and strong as he had all day.

'We will stay in the desert.' Rakhal explained the ways of his country. 'The rest of the party will return now to the palace, but it is a time for deep *tahir* for me, so you need to farewell our guests.'

'Thank you for coming.' She smiled and embraced her brother Mark. He hugged her and checked she was okay, as a brother should when his sister was grieving. He was doing so well now. He loved the land as much as Natasha did, and still worked the mines even though he was a royal now too. She was proud of him. It was so wonderful to see him strong and healthy.

Natasha then went back to her husband, who was saying goodbye to Emir and thanking him for his attendance. A dark, brooding man, Emir greeted her formally as she approached.

'How are the twins?' Natasha attempted conversation, but he hardly returned it.

'They are with the nanny.'

He kissed Rakhal on both cheeks, as was their way, and then went to his car. Natasha could see the nanny and the babies in the car behind him.

She knew what Amy had said earlier was true. They were present for duty, for appearances' sake. Not once had he looked at them.

But she could not think of Emir's pain tonight. They were driving in silence to the tent they both loved—though it would not be joyous this time. In the last three months she had grown fond of the King, and Rakhal's relationship with his father had warmed.

She took off her shoes. She was drained and exhausted, but for the first time since they had been summoned to the King's bedside they could speak properly.

'He did not suffer,' Natasha said.

'He was happy to leave.'

Rakhal surprised her, for his voice was not morose—in fact there was a pale smile.

'When everyone had said their goodbyes and I sat with him, he said he could see my mother dancing sometimes in the dust devils, and that he could see her more clearly today. It wasn't just me who saw her out in the desert.'

Natasha felt like crying, but she joined him at the low table and sat down on the floor as a maid poured water into a goblet. She drank and waited for their meal to be served.

'Now I will pray.' Rakhal rose. 'Rest if you are tired.'

'I'm actually really hungry.' She felt just a little guilty admitting it—especially when Rakhal grimaced.

'I have not explained. For two days the

country will be in the deepest of mourning.
For two days we will fast and pray. When
I return to the palace there will be a meal
at which I will preside. That is when I will
assume the role of King. For now I am to
prepare for that duty. For now we pray for
my father who is still the King.'

'I don't know if I can…' She saw him
frown, saw his features darken.

'Natasha, in so many things I do my best
to listen and to make changes where I can,
but do not disrespect me in this—for you
are disrespecting my father too, and he is
not even cold.' And he strode off to his
abode.

She followed him. 'Rakhal, please.'
There were tears in her eyes that he thought
she might be so callous, so precious, that
she would not miss a meal and keep his
ways. 'I didn't want to tell you today—not
when you are grieving—but I found out
just before we were summoned to your father.' She saw his mouth open, saw some
light in those dark eyes. 'I couldn't wait
for the moon. I saw the palace doctor this
morning—just before your father did.'
She watched as his face paled, as on this

darkest of days somehow hope shone in. 'He confirmed that I am pregnant. I honestly don't know if I am allowed to fast. Of course if I am, I will do it...'

'No!' He couldn't take it in. He should be on his knees in prayer, but instead he held her. 'It feels wrong to be happy in grief,' he admitted, 'but it feels so good to have this hope.'

He looked to her and she knew what he was thinking.

'He would rejoice.'

'He did,' Natasha whispered. 'When I farewelled him I told him.' And she was so glad that she had—just so she could have this moment. 'Of course I should have told you first, but I had only just found out myself. But he knew.' She repeated as best she could what his father's response had been.

'"My life is complete."' Rakhal translated the words his father had said to her. He knew his father was with his mother now, back with Layla and dancing in the desert. 'He kept saying that soon Alzirz would celebrate—I did not understand that he knew something I did not.'

But there would be time for smiles and

celebrations later. For now he must pray, and she must eat a light supper. For two days he would not make love to her, for two days he would pray for his father and for his country, but when he climbed into bed that night it was sweet relief to hold her—a relief he might never have known, for with the old ways this night would have been a long and lonely one.

'Are you scared to be King?' she asked as they lay together.

'I am never scared.' He answered the same way he had the first time she had asked.

'I would be.'

'I would be too,' he admitted, 'had I not found you.'

'You're going to be a wonderful ruler.'

'I know.' He was not vain. He was right. 'I am good for the people.'

'So too is Emir—as would be his girls.'

He did not respond, and tonight she chose not to push it, but one day she knew that she would.

'We will die in this bed together.' He held her. 'Or lie alone and grow old thinking of the other...' She had his heart for ever.

Deep in the night she awoke, her light supper not quite enough, but because they were in mourning she checked with him just to be sure.

'Have some of the custard.' His voice was sleepy, his arms around her. 'It is good for you.'

As was Rakhal for her.

As was Natasha for him.

And she smiled as he reached for the rope.

* * * * *